CW01099419

A note from the author

I used to teach all ages – for ages – but it became too **serious** *and rather* **sensible**…

I prefer walking my three pygmy goats on leads, feeding them with blackberry brambles and acorns.
And making my cats sing.

Don't you just love stamping in frozen puddles? The windy top of a high hill? The smell of a garden bonfire?

Have you tried eating strawberries with white pepper?
And sucking snapped off icicles?

Do you love the moon on a deep black night?
And rainbow bubbles?

I do.

Do you love listening to, reading or writing stories? Wonderful!

So do I.

THE WARRIOR TROLL

RACHAEL LINDSAY

THE WARRIOR TROLL

Nightingale Books

NIGHTINGALE PAPERBACK

A CIP catalogue record for this title is
available from the British Library.

The troll-figurine on the cover page is an original Ny Form Troll.
You will find all the Ny Form trolls at www.trollsofnorway.com

ISBN-13: 978 1 903491 47 8

Nightingale Books is an imprint of
Pegasus Elliot MacKenzie Publishers Ltd.
www.pegasuspublishers.com

First Published in 2007
Nightingale Books
Sheraton House Castle Park
Cambridge England
Printed & Bound in Great Britain

Dedication

Foor mi lovelor dearigs, Thomas Jay & Natalie Fern...
Mi treasoori foor u.
Forerver gooshty luckor mi tvo.
Kissig, kissig.

"Troll Talk" - a glossary

A

axen - axe

B

badli - bad
biggy - big
bilboorens - bilberries
boot - boat
borg - bye
brekenfasht - breakfast
brokisht - broken

C

catchen - catch/caught
cheeser - cheese
choppen - (to) chop
cloke - clock
coop - cup
crockerig - crockery

D

dearig - dear
dee - the
doori - door
dunder - (slang) dratted

E

eaten - eat/eaten
eatig - eating
es - it 's
everythingor - everything
excitig - exciting

F

fastli - faster
feelen - feeling
fetchen - (to) fetch
fior - fire
fishen - fish/fishing
fixig - fix/fixed
foor - for
"Forerver Guarderig" - forever to be
guarded
foresh - forest

G

gib - give
goingor - going
gooshty - good
guarderig - to guard/guarding

H

hab - have
helpen - help
homerig - home
hor - how

I

im - I'm/I

J

K

kissig - kiss

L

leftig - left
liker - like
lovelor - lovely
luckor - luck/lucky

M

marvellurg - marvellous

meer - me

mekken - make/s

menig - many

menor - men

mi - my

Mistig Vorter - Misty Water

moneg - money

morgy - morning

morsi(es) - mouse(mice)

mushroomer - mushrooms

musten - must

N

nay - no

needen - need

netsy - net

nics - not

O

oop - up

oor - over

oos - us

P

picken - pick /picking
pleasor - please
pussor - cat
pyor - pie

Q

R

restig - rest /sleep
ropey - rope

S

sadli - sad
smooker - smoke
soonig - soon
stoofid - stupid
strangeror - strange

T

taken - take
tay - tea
thanken - thank /s
thingors - things
todagen - today

```
treasoori - treasure

tvo - two

tworlve - twelve
```

U

```
u - you
ur - your

urnli - only

uv - you've
```

V

```
varken - wake

ve - we

verisht - very

visitori(s) - visitor(s)

vorter - water
```

W

```
weedish - weeds

willer - will

wooden - wood
```

X

Y

yart – yet

yo – yes

Z

Chapter 1

A s the sun rose, light crept through chinks in the red and white checked curtains of Hildi's kitchen, spreading its fingers slowly over the neatly-swept floor. The room was filled with a warm, pink glow. It made the wood of the hand-carved table and chairs look rosy and gave the pearly plates on the tiny dresser a pale pink shimmer.

All was still except for the tick - tick - tick of the cuckoo clock on the wall.

The small door leading to Hildi and Thom's room was slightly open and, just as the sunlight spread over the threshold –

"Cuckoo!"

The morning had begun.

Grimo, the smoky-grey cat stretched out along the foot of the bed, rolled onto his back and started to purr.

Hildi stirred first. She raised her head from the downy pillow to look at Thom and smiled a gentle troll smile. Her dimples deepened. A strand of her soft, white hair fell out of its net and she carefully tucked it in before putting a brown, weather-worn hand on Thom's shoulder.

"Gooshty morgy, Thom!" she whispered in Troll-Talk. "Varken oop!"

Thom grunted and snuffled a little and then opened his brown eyes. They softened as he turned to look at his beloved wife and he put a strong, protective arm around her.

The two of them had been together for as long as they could remember. They had met as young trolls in the forest above the fjord and they had set up home together in a small, sunny clearing. Neither knew their ages, except that Thom was somewhat younger. They were fairly sure that they were over one hundred and fifty years, but somehow age did not seem to matter. All that mattered was that they were happy and together.

With a stretch and a yawn, Thom ruffled his spiky hair and swung his little legs out of bed. He pulled on his old, green dungarees and carefully fastened the straps with strong, capable fingers. The dungarees, patched at the knee in navy-blue, were his only clothes, except for a woollen jacket, as they lived a simple life and grew warm fur when they needed it. As he stood, Thom's troll tail fell behind him, just reaching the wooden floor. The hairy end swept a spider that scurried away from Thom's broad, flat feet as he walked to the kitchen. Grimo jumped down from the bed, ears cocked, not knowing which to chase first - the spider or Thom's swishing tail.

"Wooden choppen, Hildi! Vorter fetchen!" Thom

called as he stuffed his tail into the back of his dungarees, ever wary of Grimo's painful little games at this time in the morning.

"Yo, yo, Thom," Hildi replied. "Thanken, thanken!"

As Thom left their little home in the clearing to go into the forest, Hildi sighed. He was a good Troll-Man. She took her hairnet off and replaced it with a worn, red scarf, tied under the chin. Then, after dressing in her usual simple shift, she walked with bare, hairy feet into the kitchen.

Thom was having trouble this morning. Some mornings, he decided, things went right.

And some mornings, things did not.

He had begun the day in the usual way: wood-chopping for their stove fire. This was always a quick job and never a problem.

Usually.

Today, however, Thom's axe-head was too blunt. The wooden shaft that held it had split at the second blow and the whole axe had rebounded from the log in pieces, causing Thom to duck with hairy hands over his head. His usual mild manner disappeared.

"Dunder-axen!" he yelled in annoyance and fright. "Stoofid, brokisht dunder-axen!" and his voice echoed through the dim, green forest.

After searching for the axe-head through the trees and not succeeding, Thom shrugged his furry shoulders and shook his head. He hitched up his sagging dungarees and began to pick up already broken bits of sticks and twigs, chunnering all the while. Having made a pile of firewood by their little doorstep, he collected a bucket from the side of their wooden dwelling and began to take loping troll steps down to the edge of the fjord.

The fjord was beautiful this morning. The brilliant sunshine gave the water diamond glints that sparkled and flashed. Thom bent his knees at the water's edge and scooped its icy-coldness into his bucket. Straightening up, he sighed in pleasure at the sight before him - not the fjord itself, though it was true he loved it - but his little, blue boat "Mistig Vorter" which bobbed up and down, almost begging to be taken out.

"Nay, nay, boot! Nics yart," smiled Thom, all his previous quick temper gone and he made his way up through the forest back home.

Just as he reached the pile of firewood, Thom, whose thoughts had been lost somewhere with his dear fishing boat, realised his bucket felt rather light. Peering into it, he discovered that it was empty.

"Nay vorter?" he questioned with a puzzled frown and

then, on looking closer, he saw a small hole had formed rustily in the bottom. Thom let out an exasperated snort and stomped off to his tiny workshed to find another, muttering to himself about axes and buckets, his tummy now rumbling desperately for breakfast.

Hildi, in the meantime, had tidied around the house, carefully plumping up the old, feather pillows on their rickety, wooden bed and straightening the patchwork cover. She clattered open the bedroom shutters and window, breathing in the beautiful, cold, clean air.

Grimo began to miaow and snake his way in and out of Hildi's stocky legs. He knew all the signs of breakfast time.

Hildi found his boiled fish bits in the neat kitchen and gave them to him, leaving him to enjoy them. He settled himself comfortably and purred as his pink tongue rasped around the dish. Fish-time *had* to be the best time of the day, he decided.

The cuckoo clock needed winding up next, so Hildi reached up and lovingly tended it. As she dusted the face of the clock, her cloth caught on a small, gold catch. The pretty little clock face swung open and out fell a piece of neatly folded paper.

It was the hidden Troll Map.

"Oh dearig, dearig!" Hildi sighed as her hairy knees creaked on bending to pick it up. "Thom musten fixig dee cloke catchen."

For a moment, she unfolded the ancient map and gazed at it. The sunlight from the kitchen window could almost shine through it, so thin was the paper upon which it was written.

It was very precious to Hildi and Thom and of enormous importance to all trolls. The map had been passed from generation to generation and gave details of where to find the highly valued Troll Treasure that was every troll's True Inheritance. It had been hidden, so Hildi believed, long ago at the dawn of time, when the first trolls lived in Norway. They were far greater in number then and enjoyed an undisturbed, secret life in the caves and forests high up over the fjords. Strange gems and stones had been hewn from underground passages and it was rumoured amongst trolls that they were of tremendous value and great magic. Every troll family had a copy of the map that they safe-guarded with their lives. The Troll Treasure was part of their ancestry and would neither be used nor given up unless all trolls were in desperate straits.

Hildi sighed as she folded the worn piece of paper and tucked it back behind the cuckoo clock face. Life for trolls might be difficult these days, but not *desperately* so, for there were still a few around to help each other when necessary. She had heard that some trolls even had a little money, but Hildi and Thom never had and did not understand the need for it.

Shrill squeaks brought Hildi's mind back to the jobs of the day. Tailo and Scratchen, their pet mice, were demanding to be fed now that Grimo had finished his fish and had jumped out of the bedroom window for his morning forest hunt. The mice knew better than to make a noise before Grimo had been fed.

Tailo was a cantankerous little creature with bright eyes and sharp teeth in amongst a fat ball of brown fur. Scratchen, on the other hand, was smaller, thinner and as black as elderberries. He was constantly scritch-scratching around his neck with his sharp claws. They had adopted Hildi and Thom one evening as the trolls ate bread and cheese by the fire. It seemed to Hildi that Tailo had barely stopped eating since. They had no idea where the mice had come from and presumed they had arrived on a boat. They were definitely not troll-mice because of the way they spoke.

"Feed us! Feed us!" Tailo now shrieked from their safe corner on the dresser, where Grimo was forbidden to jump. "Get the bread out, Hildi! Never mind that spoilt brat cat! My ribs are sticking through! Can't visiting mice get any breakfast around here?"

"Visitoris! Hah!" Hildi called back. Tailo and Scratchen had been the longest-staying visitors *she* had ever had. It was many months ago that the mice had turned up. They had both been weak and thin then and Thom had caught them easily, but they were wild, scratchy and not at all happy. Hildi decided sensibly that it was better to leave the mice on the floor and feed them, hoping they might feel friendlier afterwards. At the sight of the bread and cheese, the little visitors had calmed down and Tailo and Scratchen became part of the family. Their bad manners did not improve but the trolls accepted this with gentle grace.

Tailo and Scratchen were no more pleasant this morning. Hildi took no notice of their rudeness. She found some dark rye bread and the crusty coating of some cheese and left Tailo tucking in with gusto, whilst thinner Scratchen sneaked bits away from him whenever he could.

Thom had finished at last. He burst into the kitchen with a bundle of firewood under his arm and fresh, cold water slip-slapping in a bucket, swinging from one hand. Within minutes, the fire in the old, black stove was lit and some nettle tea was brewing. Hildi told Thom about the cuckoo clock catch and Thom busily secured it, making sure it would not open so easily. The cured ham, rye bread and blackberries were placed carefully on the sturdy, wooden table and two mugs of steaming nettle tea poured out.

"Eaten ur brekenfasht, Thom," Hildi said, sitting down.

"Yo, yo, Hildi. Thanken, thanken!" Thom sat beside her and smiled a broad, dimpled smile and it seemed that the whole of their cosy home was filled with love, the fragrance of pine and of nettle tea. As they munched and sipped, with Grimo now at their feet watching for any mouse movement from the dresser, neither Thom nor Hildi had any idea of the dreadful events about to unfold or of the terrible turmoil about to shatter their peaceful lives.

Chapter 2

When Thom had wiped the last smears of black-berry juice from around his hairy lips and drained his cup, he rose from the table and announced he was going to mend his fishing lines and nets outside their little shed.

Tailo, now completely stuffed, had long since curled up in a piece of old, woolly blanket in a corner of the dresser. He made mouse grunts as he slept and chomped his yellow teeth on imaginary ears of corn. Scratchen sat on his haunches next to him, having the occasional scratch and scowling. Tailo had left only a few crumbs of bread for him as usual and Scratchen was very hungry.

It was always the same.

Hildi would give them a meal and Tailo would dive onto it before Scratchen had a chance. Eventually, when full, he would move away, leaving a few crumbs that he was too lazy to be bothered with.

"Greedy Rat-Face!" Scratchen muttered to himself as he chewed a dry, left-over crumb. "I hope you feel really sick now!" But he had to admit to himself that

Tailo did not *look* particularly uncomfortable as he slept in the soft blanket on the dresser.

"I'll teach him a lesson one day!" Scratchen promised himself as he cleaned his whiskers meticulously - just in case there was anything worth eating left on them.

Hildi cleared the table and threw some more twigs on the smoking stove fire, making it blaze and crackle. Then she settled herself with her dried flowers and leaves, to make her troll pictures. This was her favourite pastime and her pictures were truly beautiful. They had a magical quality that was all her own.

Today, she was going to make a forest picture since she had done two water pictures recently. These were now stored with the others at the bottom of the dresser ready for exchange at a later date. The fish fins and tails she used had been a little smelly at first which was rather off-putting but, after drying, they were fine and looked wonderful among the dried weeds and plants on a background of turquoise blue. The scales glinted silver and made the pictures shine. Hildi tried to keep the fragrance *in* her forest pictures, though. She sprinkled each one liberally with Essence of Pine and used some of the herbs that hung from the low ceiling over the stove.

The pictures were used when Hildi and Thom really needed something from the Big People - a new bucket or axe for example. Since they had no money, the pictures were used in exchange for the goods they needed and they were so unusual that they never had any shortage of takers. Hildi had a gift for art and loved snipping, arranging and sticking.

"Fishen in 'Mistig Vorter' boot, Hildi!" Thom called through the door. "Netsy fixig. Gooshty borg!"

"Yo, yo, Thom! Gooshty luckor. Fishen foor tay!" smiled Hildi. "Im picken bilboorens soonig in foresh foor pyor. Gooshty borg!"

Tailo had woken up when Thom opened the door to call goodbye. He was not a happy mouse. He was sleepy and cross.

"Why doesn't he just *GO*?" Tailo grumbled loudly as he heaved his fat body over to the other side of the blanket bed. "They spend so much time talking rubbish Troll-Talk to each other that the day will be over before Thom has a chance to get his daft, little boat out!"

"You're just in a bad mood because you've eaten too much!" replied Scratchen with a certain amount of satisfaction.

"Pah!" spat back Tailo with as much force as he could muster on a full stomach. "You're such a weedy specimen that you don't need as much food as me! I need to maintain my magnificent body and athletic muscle tone!" and he swelled out his brown, furry chest in pride.

Scratchen was not at all impressed and dived forwards, paws and scratchy claws outstretched. He gave

Tailo's belly such a thump that all the air he had taken in came whistling out and left him coughing and spluttering. Grimo, on hearing the squeaking and commotion from the dresser, could bear it no longer. He leapt up with claws out and ears back, landing with an almighty crash amongst the beautiful, pearly plates.

They fell smashing to the floor.

Grimo lost his grip in all the confusion and missed both mice, ending up in a heap with all the broken crockery.

"GRIMO! GRIMO!" Hildi yelled in anguish. "Nay, nay! Mi lovelor crockerig!"

Grimo hung his head low and slunk to the open door where Thom stood. He was helped out by Thom's hairy foot and went to lick himself in a quiet spot so he could recover. It was always *so* embarrassing to misjudge a move like that!

Tailo and Scratchen had forgotten their fight and, after the initial shock when they had clung to each other in fright, they had a friendly competition to see who could make the rudest face at Grimo through the window.

Hildi was very upset. She had been very fond of those plates and knew it would take a lot of picture - making to replace them. Thom put his loving arm around her and chuffed her under the chin. Together they tidied up.

When Hildi was feeling better, Thom left to go fishing. Hildi continued with her work, wondering whether she could use some of the bilberries she was going to pick, in her forest picture.

Mistig Vorter seemed to bob its greeting at Thom as he reached the water's edge. He was laden down with fishing net and lines and it took him a few minutes to settle himself with tackle in the little boat. Taking up the oars, he rowed *dip - plip* to the middle of the fjord, his strong arms moving slowly and rhythmically. He had decided to fish further out today because the water was so calm and there was barely a breath of wind. After ten minutes' rowing, he stopped and rested his arms on the oars.

The view around him was truly magnificent. No matter how many years he lived, he would never take this for granted. The blue of the water reflected the sky. The forests up the mountainside were vivid green.

"Marvellurg!" Thom whispered to his boat, patting the sides.

Then, with a quick flick, he flung his net into the water and let it sink right down into the depths. He secured the rope from it to one side of the boat and then cast his fishing line from the other.

"Im feelen luckor, Mistig! Verisht luckor todagen,"

Thom announced. He lay back in his dear little boat, listening to the water lapping against it and closed his gentle, brown eyes.

What bliss!

Within minutes, there was a tug at his line and, blinking in the bright light, Thom pulled in a large fish. It landed in the bottom of Mistig Vorter, flipped this way and that for a moment and then lay still. Thom was delighted! Not only was the fish a good size and would make them three fine meals, but also the fins and scales were a shining silver-blue, ideal for Hildi's pictures. Thom cast his line again and again until, by the end of the afternoon, he had a dozen, beautiful, fresh fish.

He had never had such luck!

"Marvellurg, gooshty fishen todagen!" he grinned to himself and his mouth watered at the thought of his meal to come.

Because trolls always believe in the balance of things, Thom was convinced that his good luck in fishing was a direct result of their bad luck this morning, with axe, bucket and plates. He did not realise that those incidents were not bad luck at all compared with what was yet to come...

The forest was bathed in a dim, green light that day. It was cool and shady. The air hung heavy with the smell of pine and wild mushrooms. Hildi picked her way deftly through the trees along well-worn paths, carrying her old basket on one arm.

"Hildi picked her way deftly through the trees..."

Tailo and Scratchen sat in the basket as they always did when fruit was being collected. Hildi enjoyed their company and it kept them safe from Grimo.

These trips always pleased Tailo because he liked to make a separate pile of the best berries for himself, although he pretended this was not the case. Whenever the pile got too big, he would wolf the berries down and then select some more while he caught his breath from the sudden bout of scoffing. Scratchen knew what he was doing and was not at all surprised. Scratchen was content to nibble on the odd berry he managed to get to before Tailo did. That way, he got a few to eat, at least.

"I'll look after that one, Hildi!" Tailo would squeak, as a particularly plump bilberry fell into the basket. "We don't want it to get squashed, do we?" and he licked his greedy lips, rubbing his round belly as he did so.

Hildi did not reply. She was well used to his greediness and it didn't bother her. There was always plenty of food to be gathered in the forest, if you had a troll's eye and knew where to look.

"What about the mushrooms today, Hildi? We can't live on bilberries alone, you know! A mouse has to have Variety in his diet!" Tailo said the word 'variety' as if it were a different kind of berry that could be picked and tossed into the basket with the others.

"Nay, nay, Tailo! Nics todagen. In morgy picken mushroomer... yo, yo, in morgy..." Hildi's voice trailed off as she scanned the bushes for fruit. She absentmindedly patted Tailo's head so that he bobbed up and down. That, together with the swinging basket, made him feel quite ill and he wasted no time in saying so.

"Stop it. STOP IT! You're making me feel sick! I'm not a dog to be patted, you know, Hildi! I'm going to be sick in your basket and it's all your fault! All the little bits will get stuck in the wicker work!" Tailo groaned dramatically and put a paw over his mouth.

"Nay! Nay!" Hildi smiled, quite undisturbed by Tailo's drama. "Uv eaten too menig bilboorens!"

"Bilberries?" Tailo repeated, trying to appear incredulous. "Me? Pah! I don't even *like* them that much! I've not eaten *one*!"

"More like *fifty-one*, you great Fat-Rat!" retorted Scratchen from the depths of the basket, as he scratched at a particularly tickly spot.

Tailo thought it better not to continue this argument because it is very difficult to think of clever things to say when you are feeling sick. Instead he turned his brown, pouty nose up in the air to look snooty, showing his purple, bilberry-stained mouth and teeth as he did so.

His belly bulged.

Unfortunately, the throwing back of his head made him lose his balance and he fell onto his back amongst his special pile of berries, squashing them all flat so the juice dripped through the basket onto the forest floor.

"Now look what you have made me do!" Tailo squeaked indignantly and he began to groom his dripping, purple fur with his tiny, purple tongue.

Scratchen was delighted.

As Hildi began her return journey, she managed to stifle a bubble of laughter that rose in her throat and turn it into a cough to save Tailo any further embarrassment. She knew that if Tailo thought she was laughing at him, he would sulk for days and have to be coaxed out of it with all sorts of special treats. There were times when he could be a Very Difficult Mouse.

Having landed the last of his fish, Thom began to pull in his net. He had caught so many fish with his line that he really had not needed to use both methods. The net felt heavy today. He could not believe that he had caught yet *more* fish.

He began to worry about how to transport them all home. Thom had never had a day like this before.

Slowly, slowly, up came the net.

Strange... there seemed to be no movement in it, so the weight could not be fish. Thom peered into the water. All he could see were green weeds where the net had dragged along the bottom as the boat bobbed.

"Urnli weedish!" he exclaimed, as the main part of the net broke the surface.

It was just as Thom was about to untangle and gather it in for next time, that he noticed something.

The Something seemed to have an oilskin covering and there was a flash of a gold buckle, but then the weeds shifted and floated over it.

Had there really been anything there?

Thom fumbled about in the weeds, but the net was so heavy he felt in danger of falling overboard as he could not hold it with one hand. He peered once more into the depths and pulled his net against the side of the boat.

This time he could see the object more clearly. As he pushed the weeds away, the top of a large casket was uncovered.

A simple, heavy, old casket.

It had a weather-proof, oiled coating and was fastened with a single, large buckle. Thom heaved it into Mistig Vorter, curious to know the contents. It landed with a dull thud.

Thom felt a thrill of excitement as he rowed back to the shore. He had really been blessed that day. All that fish and now this! How lucky!

How wrong could a troll be?

Chapter 3

H ildi was just taking some brown, crusty bread out of the oven and placing it on the windowsill to cool, when Thom came briskly up the path, six large fish strung together and slung over each shoulder.

"Hildi! Hildi!" he cried as he burst in through the small door. "Tworlve fishen todagen! Tworlve!"

Hildi looked at the beautiful fish that Thom was unloading onto the table.

"Oh verisht gooshty Thom!" she exclaimed in delight. "Im willer smooker fishen oor fior. Kissig, kissig Thom! Thanken!" and Hildi clapped her hands together, kissing Thom's hot, brown face.

Tailo's head emerged from the piece of woollen blanket on the dresser, where he had been dozing his bilberries away, and he grimaced at this display of affection and thanks.

"Here we go again!" he muttered to Scratchen in disgust. "All this 'kissig' business. Why can't they leave each other *alone*? I can't be doing with it."

Scratchen thought it was pretty soppy too but was not going to say so because he *never* agreed with Tailo.

Tailo was just about to dig deeper into his snuggly

bed when he caught a waft of fish coming from the table. He peered over his blanket, his beady eyes suddenly alert and his nose twitching.

"Food!" he squeaked. He scrambled out of bed, almost fell off the dresser and scurried up a table leg.

"Nay! Nay, Tailo!" Hildi cried and gathered the grumbling mouse up in her hands just as he was getting ready to sink his teeth into a fish. "Nics foor morsi! Cheeser foor morsies, nics fishen!"

"But I *like* eating fish," squawked Tailo, struggling to get free from Hildi's grip.

"*U* liker eatig *everythingor*!" laughed Thom as Hildi gently dropped the objecting mouse outside the kitchen window and shut it after him.

Thom hurriedly explained to Hildi all about his day's fishing and how he had found something else. Announcing he would be back in a few minutes, he left Hildi gutting the fish ready for smoking over their wood stove and took large troll steps down to Mistig Vorter. Tailo spent a mad few moments scratching at the kitchen door and then, deciding that all he was doing was wearing out his claws, he started to look for a chink in the wall to creep through. By the time he had found Hildi and Thom's open bedroom window and got in again, the fish were hung over the fire in a special, wooden cradle. The smoke wisped through and filled the room with a tasty, kippery smell before weaving its way up through the twisted chimney and out into the forest. Delicious – but no chance!

And anyway, THAT CAT was guarding it very seriously, his tail twitching, his eyes and ears alert. No mouse was going to get *his* fish!

Thom smelled the smoke as he staggered up the path with the casket he had netted that day. He had not yet opened it and, for the first time, he feared the disappointment of finding it empty - or full of stones. Still, he thought, it would make a lovely workbox for Hildi's picture-making items.

The table was clear again as Thom lumbered into the kitchen, so he could thump the casket down without having to wait. This was just as well because his arms could not have held it much longer and his strong, hairy hands were slipping.

"Hor excitig!" exclaimed Hildi when she saw it. Her old eyes shone and she shuffled to the kitchen drawer to get a strong knife with which to break the buckle. Years in the water had weakened the metal and it gave way easily, falling onto the table with a soft thud.

Tailo, annoyed at having missed the fish, watched from a discreet distance with interest. What would the contents of the casket be? His belly rumbled hopefully and his nose strained forwards to sniff as hard as it could.

Although the buckle was indeed off, the casket lid seemed well sealed and did not want to move. Thom took the knife and scratched at the join between the domed lid and base. The slimy algae were easily removed, revealing a wax seal all around.

"Aha!" shouted Thom - unnecessarily, Tailo thought, because it made him jump and disturbed his nose concentration. He watched closely as Thom took the point of his knife all the way around the seal of the lid and dug in deep. Long, thin curls of wax fell from the casket onto the table. Tailo considered chewing one but then decided they looked a bit sticky and might glue his teeth together, which would be a disaster.

Once the wax was removed, the oily skin over the casket could be peeled off and Thom slowly pushed the lid back. Scratchen peered over his blanket. He even stopped scratching for a moment and Grimo actually took his eyes off the smoked fish...

They all held their breath as they looked in...

Curious treasures lay before their eyes:

Silver crosses and pendants; oval brooches in ancient gold, silver and bronze; arm rings and neck rings, made from silver coins and engraved with strange writing.

Hildi and Thom looked at each other with puzzled expressions. They did not know what to make of it all. Grimo lost interest and returned his gaze to the smoking fish, wondering if he could swipe a piece whilst no one was looking.

"Verisht strangeror!" mused Thom as he pulled the odd items from the casket and placed them carefully on the table.

Hildi pulled out a plaited neckband made from thick, dull, golden wires. A heavy hammer-shaped piece hung from it. It looked strong and manly. Hildi did not like it at all.

"Nics verisht lovelor, Thom!" she said, grimacing.

"Not very tasty either!" muttered Tailo, unable to hide his disappointment at the contents of the box. "Isn't it time for tea?"

"Nics yart, Tailo..." replied Thom, his voice trailing off as he examined the rest of the find.

There were large, bronze keys for unknown doors or even other caskets. They clanked as they were unloaded onto the table. Small bronze and silver figurines jostled amongst necklaces of coloured glass beads. Hildi held one of the necklaces up to the light. The colours were deep: sea greens, wine reds, amber yellows, and the coloured light which shone through them danced and flashed across the table as Hildi let them gently sway in her hands.

"Oh, lovelor, Thom! Foor meer, pleasor?" and Hildi

passed one of the glass necklaces to Thom so that he could fasten it around her neck. Her little, old face shone with pleasure. The gold and bronze and silver meant nothing to her, she loved only pretty colours.

Whilst the two trolls were busily engaged, Grimo decided to go for the fish. The cradle swung tantalizingly above his head, fish tails poking through. Balancing on the basket of wood at the fireplace, he stretched up one eager paw and swiped at it. The cradle went swinging wildly backwards and forwards, creaking on its black, iron hook. Grimo withdrew his paw and wobbled for a moment, losing his balance on the pile of wood. Then, when the cradle of fish was still, he stretched up for another try.

Scratchen, from his elevated position on the dresser, could see exactly what was going on. He never missed a trick. He smiled his best crafty smile, drew in a deep breath and crept towards a teacup, which stood further down the shelf.

Grimo glanced at Hildi and Thom. They were still admiring the necklace.

All clear.

He balanced back on his hind legs, stretching up...

Just as Grimo was about to take another swipe at the cradle, Scratchen pushed the teacup off the dresser -

CRASH!

A thousand teacup pieces shattered the silence.

Grimo nearly leapt out of his skin. He lost his balance on the wood basket and fell forwards onto the edge of the fire. With a fearsome screech, he hurtled backwards and collided with a table leg, banging his head and ended up on his back, legs akimbo.

"Scratchen! Mi lovelor coop! Grimo! Stoofid pussor!" cried Hildi in dismay, not knowing quite which calamity to be the most upset about, the cup or the cat.

Scratchen dived for cover and lay low. He was very pleased with himself. That evened things up a bit. Grimo obviously did not like getting a shock any more than *they* had that morning, when he had tried to catch them on the dresser.

And for the second time that day, Grimo was ejected unceremoniously from the house, feeling rather dazed and not quite knowing what had happened to him. He was left outside, nursing his head and licking his singed, front paw.

Hildi and Thom continued to unpack the casket. The figurines were placed on the table top, which was getting fairly crammed by now. They were strange figures with twisted faces and oddly shaped bodies. Like the ugly hammer ornament on the plaited, gold neckband, they seemed to have a strength that the trolls were vaguely uncomfortable about.

One small statue was different from the rest.

It was no larger but it stood on a gold base. The face

was truly terrible; a beast unknown to Hildi and Thom with a bird's beak and great, piercing eyes. Matted hair fell about his shoulders, over his broad chest to his waist. He held a great spear in one hand whilst the other was raised to the sky. The legs and feet were that of a hoofed animal, thickset and standing firm. Around the base were ravens with meat falling from their hooked beaks and two, lean wolves, tongues lolling from their mouths.

The base of the statue held an inscription and some strange, scratched lines:

"WODAN, ID EST FUROR"

Neither Hildi nor Thom knew the meaning of this. They read the words and looked at each other questioningly.

They were to understand this in the fullness of time...

Somehow, the trolls felt that this figure should not be piled up with the others. They felt uneasy about treating it like the rest. Thom placed it with care on the top dresser shelf, safely away from cat and mice.

His hands shook as he did so.

He did not understand why.

Under a bag of old coins, not all whole - some had chinks cut out of them, which spoiled the strange writing on them - and a similar bag of heavy rings (too large for Hildi's fingers, even if she *had* wanted to wear them) were six knives and beakers and bowls. They were not particularly pretty but, Hildi decided, they were functional and goodness knows, she needed them! She put them to wash in her little troll sink. Strangely, there were no spoons or forks, which upset Hildi because she was always meticulously neat and she would have liked a matching set.

Towards the bottom of the casket, to Thom's amazement, they found two swords, several spearheads and two fine axe-heads. Thom gave a whoop of delight! He ran his finger down the edge of an axe-head and found it was sharp. It was even better than the one he had lost in the forest that morning.

All that remained in the casket was a large helmet with a plaque on it. The picture on the plaque was of the figure now standing on the top shelf of the dresser.

Thom, pleased with his axe-head, grinned still further, his dimples showing. With slow deliberation, he placed the helmet on his spiky, hairy head. To his surprise, it almost fitted him, as the spare space in the helmet was taken up by his fuzzy hair. He took hold of one of the ancient swords and stood before Hildi, warrior-like.

"Oh good grief!" exclaimed Tailo, when he saw this.

"Look at him! I've really seen it all now! Big, bad Thom-the-Troll in his fancy dress!"

Scratchen joined him and looked.

"Hmm," he said, thoughtfully, "actually, he *does* look pretty fierce - for a troll, that is..."

"Thom couldn't be fierce if he tried," sneered Tailo. "He doesn't scare me!"

"Oh, yes? And I suppose you're *never* scared, are you?" replied Scratchen in a bored sort of voice.

"Well, a mouse of *my* stature and physique doesn't *have* to be scared, actually!" and Tailo drew himself up in an important manner.

"You seemed rather scared this morning when THAT CAT launched himself at us!"

Scratchen tittered at Tailo's cross face. Tailo did not like to be caught out like that and was not amused.

"I wasn't scared!" he squeaked in annoyance. "I only clutched you to protect you and I must say it's about time you thanked me for it!" and Tailo sat back, well pleased with the way he had twisted things round.

"Rubbish!" retorted Scratchen, not impressed, and he turned his back on Tailo to look down once more at Thom.

Hildi was not happy, but Thom had been so wrapped up in his appearance that he had not noticed. He had stomped round the table with his sword and helmet, feeling very pleased with himself.

"Nay, Thom! Nics gooshty luckor!" Hildi cried out.

Thom stopped stomping and sighed. Hildi was always thinking things would be bad luck. She was always *so* cautious. But something about Hildi's dear face made him follow her gaze, which fell upon the small statue on the top shelf of the dresser.

The statue seemed to be shaking.

Thom quickly took off the helmet, looking guilty like a naughty child.

The statue became still.

Perhaps they had imagined it.

Perhaps it had been Thom's stomping that had set it off.

Hildi took the helmet from Thom and put it on the windowsill. She lifted a plant with softly-falling stems and leaves into it, lovingly, and glanced up at the statue.

The quivering had stopped.

It remained motionless.

Together the trolls cleared the table, putting the strange objects here and there in the little home. Hildi washed the bowls and beakers and knives and set them on the dresser.

"Don't put them here!" came a familiar voice. "Not unless they've got some food in them, that is!"

Hildi shook her head and smiled. Always hungry, that mouse! Come to think of it, after all that excitement, she felt fairly hungry herself.

Chapter 4

A ll was well with the trolls until the Big Person came.

That day, the morning dawned bright and crisp. Not a sound was to be heard in the forest outside Thom and Hildi's home, except for the slight rustle of the wind in the trees.

Inside, everyone slept.

Tailo and Scratchen were curled up together in their old piece of blanket, dreaming mouse dreams. Scratchen twitched suddenly as he felt a scratch coming on, but managed to sleep through it. Their legs and paws were entwined and Scratchen's head rested against Tailo's belly, which gurgled hungrily as he ate his dream nuts and berries.

Thom had his arm around Hildi and they both slept peacefully, her head on his hairy chest. As he took deep breaths in, some of Hildi's downy-soft hair fluttered up to his nostrils and then it floated down again to rest on her hairnet. She was smiling a sweet, gentle smile in her sleep, lost in mists of troll recipes for herb soup and fish pie.

Thom snuffled and rubbed his nose vigorously as an

extra piece of Hildi's hair escaped from her net and tickled him. Hildi mumbled something and turned over, staying asleep herself but disturbing Grimo who lay at her feet. He gave a lazy, warm stretch and started to dig his claws into the patchwork quilt, catching the cotton threads and puckering them up.

SNAP!

Outside, there was a sudden noise, quick and light - the snapping of a twig on the ground. Grimo's ears pricked up and his eyes became round and saucerish. He turned his gaze to the window, even though it was shuttered up, and watched warily.

CRACK!

Another snap of a twig and the sound of a footfall on the forest floor. Grimo's tail flicked this way and that for a moment, but no other sound was to be heard.

Hildi and Thom slept on.

Grimo, still rather unsettled, rested his head back on his front paws but kept his eyes open and ears alert.

Footsteps around the side of the house, quiet and careful...

Scratchen awoke. He was not sure what had disturbed him, but he thought that something had. He raised his back leg up to his ear and began his morning scratch.

Kick-kick-kick, all around his ear and neck, tickle-tickle, scratch-scratch.

For a second, something caught his eye.

Was that a face he had seen peering through a gap in the kitchen curtain?

Scratchen gave Tailo a nudge. His little, sharp elbow dug into Tailo's belly and made him wake up with a jump and a frown.

"Tailo! I've just seen something!" Scratchen whispered.

Tailo was not in a good mood. "So what?" he hissed back. "I was in the middle of a wonderful dream - the pastry crust just melting in my mouth - and *you* wake me to tell me that you have seen something! Well it had better be *GOOD!* At least as good as eating nut pie! What was it? Something to eat, I hope?"

Scratchen shuffled uncomfortably in the blanket. He was not at all sure that Tailo would be interested in a face at the window. He was just about to make up a different story when

BLAM! BLAM!

- there were two loud blows at the door.

Grimo, already a bit twitchy, screeched in shock and leapt to his feet, claws still in the patchwork quilt, ripping a section as he did so. He dived for cover under the bed, growling, his fur standing up on end and his tail lashing to and fro.

Hildi clutched Thom in panic and Thom was quick to hold her. It was very rare that someone should knock at their door.

The Someone rattled the door handle.

"Yes, yes!" Thom called out, abandoning his usual Troll-Talk as he grabbed his dungarees and tucked his tail in. It was always wise to try to hide any sign of troll-ness with strangers. It always made them too curious.

At the sound of Thom's voice, the door handle was left alone.

"NO WORRIES!" the visitor bellowed from outside.

Scratchen and Tailo buried their heads in their blanket and trembled. The booming voice frightened them. The *visitor* may not have any worries but *they* certainly had.

After reassuring Hildi, Thom answered the door.

There, before him, stood two great walking boots. Thom's eyes travelled slowly upwards.

Great tree trunk legs, clad in leather, grew out of the boots.

Thom's eyes moved up further.

The Big Person towered over him, making him feel afraid and uncertain. He had a fiery-red beard and a mop of unkempt hair. Over one shoulder he carried a haversack - and in his other hand... in his other hand... in his other hand... he carried a GUN!

Thom gulped.

Grimo took one look at the stranger and shot outside

through his legs.

"Hah! Looks like your cat's not too pleased to see me!" grinned the Big Person, but held out his great hand to Thom in a friendly gesture of greeting.

Tailo and Scratchen pricked up their ears. It was not often that they heard someone speak their own language. They lost their fright and looked at the visitor with new interest.

"He can't be *all* bad!" Scratchen whispered. "He talks like us!"

"I never thought he *was* bad!" retorted Tailo, looking superior as usual. "I hope you don't think I was scared just then!"

"My dear Tailo! Of course not! You were trembling with cold, weren't you?" replied Scratchen with a knowing smile on his little black-whiskered face.

Tailo made no reply. He thought it was best not to continue this conversation. Instead, he looked at the stranger and Thom as if he were very intent on what *they* were saying and had not heard Scratchen.

Thom relaxed.

The Big Person was pleasant and friendly. He explained that he was walking and hunting in the forest and had lost his way. He had come across their dwelling and thought straight away that he would see if anyone could help him.

Grimo, listening outside, was not convinced.

Why had he been creeping and snooping?

Did he think that there was nobody in when he banged at the door and then tried the handle?

Hildi joined Thom at the door and, hearing a friendly voice, immediately invited the stranger into their little home and offered him breakfast. It had been a long time since they had had anyone to visit them and it was quite a change to see a new face. She was excited and pleased. Within minutes, there was food on the table and the three were seated. Tailo thought things were definitely looking up and his mouth watered at the prospect of some juicy tit-bits coming his way. His belly rumbled desperately for breakfast. That dream about nut pie had just whetted his appetite and he was longing for something tasty.

"These are very unusual bowls and beakers," commented the stranger, pleasantly enough. "How did you come by them?"

Thom was pleased he had noticed them and eagerly told him about the fishing of the other day.

"There were many marvellous - and strange - things in my net!" Thom explained, gesturing around the room. Hildi joined in.

"Yes! Many lovely things! Not only crockery!" and she placed her hand on her precious, new, glass bead necklace.

The Big Person gasped as he saw it and seemed

mesmerised by its flashing colours. He had grown quite pale. Hildi, chatting away, did not notice and went on to grumble that there were no spoons or forks to go with the knives they had found. The stranger seemed to snap out of his daze.

"Well, they never used spoons or forks - they ate everything with knives," he blurted out in sudden excitement. Hildi and Thom looked confused all of a sudden.

"Don't you *know*?" the man asked, looking from Hildi to Thom. "These are VIKING treasures! You have fished out a VIKING CASKET! One of their long boats must have sunk in the fjord, many years ago, and you have dredged your net along the bottom and caught all this – this..." the Big Person seemed stuck for words, "...this FORTUNE!"

Hildi and Thom looked at each other. Neither could understand the visitor's excitement. Surely a bit of old junk like this could not be worth a fortune? And anyway, so what if it was? They had no need for money - they did not see the point of it.

Grimo had crept back in during this conversation. He thought he had better investigate. He cautiously sniffed the great boots as he positioned himself under the table.

This man even *smelled* suspicious.

Grimo peered into an open corner of the haversack, which was at his side. Bottles and knives and bait for catching animals lay in a jumble.

One bottle's label could be seen quite clearly:

DANGER

RAT POISON

A blue powder was inside. Grimo shuddered. This visitor was certainly no friend to animals. As he waited under the table for bits of smoked fish, the stranger reached down and loosened a buckle on his boot. The blue powder was lying thickly under his fingernails. Grimo backed away from him. He was certainly not going to eat any fish bits from *his* hands!

As they ate, Hildi and Thom talked about other objects. They showed the visitor the plaited neckband made from thick, dull, golden wires with the heavy hammer-shaped piece hanging from it. The man recognised it at once.

"That's Thor's hammer! And look at the *gold*! Only the very wealthy Vikings had gold! Most had necklaces and brooches made from bronze or not at all! This really is *MOST* unusual!"

Hildi sniffed and tossed the neckband onto the dresser. "Unusual it may be, but it is ugly. Manly and too strong, somehow," she said.

As the neckband clattered onto the dresser, Hildi glanced quickly up at the small statue on the top shelf, the one that seemed to hold so much power.

It was quite still.

But was it watching them?

Hildi was certainly not going to get that one down to show to the visitor. The least said about *that* one, the better.

Tailo was gnashing his teeth. All this jabbering was all very well but Hildi did not seem to realise that she had not yet fed the two mice. He glared at Grimo with as much hate as he could muster on an empty stomach and gnashed his teeth until he thought of a plan.

"Scratchen?" he wheedled, before long. Scratchen looked up.

"There are a lot of fish bits being dropped on the

floor for THAT CAT and he doesn't seem to be eating them all. I've got a brill idea. You *are* hungry, aren't you?"

Scratchen had to admit that he was, *very* hungry in fact.

"How about you distracting THAT CAT whilst I nip in and grab some of the fish bits for us?" Tailo suggested and he licked his greedy lips in anticipation of a good meal.

Scratchen thought this over. There was no doubt whatsoever that this would be a trick on Tailo's part. He was certain that Tailo would not save any fish for him but would gobble it all up himself. Added to this was the fact that Scratchen had a Seriously Risky job in distracting Grimo so that Tailo could dive in there. However, Scratchen was not a stupid mouse and he also knew that if THAT CAT was actually *leaving* some of the fish, there *must* be something wrong with it. Scratchen decided to observe the situation more closely and so he played for time.

"It sounds a bit dodgy to me," he replied to Tailo, his eyes keenly watching Grimo's movements.

"Listen, pal," replied Tailo in a threatening tone of voice, "we're not going to get any breakfast today unless you cooperate. Those daft trolls are far too wrapped up in this visitor to remember *us*! So, if you know what's good for you, you'd better get down there and start distracting!"

Scratchen, absolutely unconcerned about Tailo's threats, had seen all he needed to see. It was obvious that Grimo was only leaving the fish thrown down to him from the Big Person.

He must have a good reason for it.

And so, to settle a few old scores, Scratchen went along with Tailo's plan, even though he knew that Tailo was only trying to trick him out of yet more food.

Thom was involved in showing the stranger his bag of Viking coins as Scratchen scrambled down the dresser onto the kitchen floor.

"Aha!" exclaimed the man, picking up a coin and holding it to the light. "The writing on this coin is in Arabic. It tells us when and where it was minted."

"Minted?" queried Hildi. The only mint *she* had ever heard of was that which grew outside their little dwelling and which now hung, drying, over the small stove. She was rapidly losing understanding of the visitor's conversation. It seemed to her that he was so wrapped up in their so-called treasure that he was talking mainly to himself. She scratched her head and sighed. She was getting a little tired of this Big Person.

"Yes," the man continued, "and look! Here are some coins that are missing pieces because they were used as part payment when a whole coin was too much." The stranger's eyes were wild and excited. His fingers were sweaty and the coins slipped through them. He started to count them busily, no longer aware that he was a visitor in this gentle troll home.

"Did you find a Vendel helmet?" the man asked, eagerly.

"Vendel?" questioned Thom, looking puzzled. Then his face cleared. "Ah! Yes, the helmet! Actually..."

Hildi shot a glance of warning at Thom. After Thom's brief game with the helmet before, she was not keen to mess with it any more. She did not trust the statue.

"Actually - er - no!" Thom continued hurriedly. "No helmets!"

The stranger eyed him for a moment, as if unconvinced.

"No! No Vendel helmets!" repeated Thom with more conviction as he avoided the man's gaze and pushed some more coins his way.

"No worries," replied the stranger, absorbed once more.

Scratchen decided now was the moment. He stuck his tongue out at Grimo and then turned around, showing his bottom before scampering through the table legs and across the kitchen floor.

Grimo was absolutely astonished.

For a second or two he could not believe his eyes. Then, furious at Scratchen's nerve, he gave chase. Tailo seized his opportunity and made a grab for the bits of fish, which lay at the Big Person's great feet. He stuffed as much as he could into his fat chops and then hid just before Grimo returned.

Scratchen joined him, panting and trembling a little. He hoped this was going to be worth it. He was going to be extremely mad if there was nothing wrong with the fish. However, to go along with the plan, he made a big act of grumbling at Tailo for not saving him any. The two mice retreated to the dresser. Tailo, satisfied with his trick, chortled to himself.

It was only when they were back in the safety of their blanket that he noticed Scratchen was also smiling. This unnerved Tailo a little. Scratchen refused to say why he looked so pleased with himself; he just told Tailo that he would find out soon enough.

Grimo had given up the chase. He was more concerned about the stranger and he wanted to keep his eyes and ears open. He wondered whether he could sharpen his claws on the man's legs, but decided he might get thrown out again. Instead, he strained to listen to the conversation.

"No, no! It does not interest us! We do not use it!" Thom was saying, as he refused the visitor's offer of money for the Viking items. He shook his head and stood up from the table.

The Big Person rose too. He towered over Thom and threw some more money on the table. The coins scattered and spun, knocking against the Viking bowls and beakers.

Hildi looked at the money, puzzled. She did not understand money. It was the bowls and beakers they needed; and the axe-head; and the helmet was a useful plant pot; and the Viking coins would make good fishing net weights. They had polished many items and they were attractive around the house. The heavier figurines were good to weigh down her pressed flowers and the brooches clamped her herb stems together beautifully. She clutched her pretty necklace in her old, brown hand. *Nobody* was having that!

Grimo watched the stranger's face harden for an instant and then, almost immediately, it relaxed once more. Hildi and Thom did not seem to notice. They were walking to the door, followed by the man.

Tailo shuffled uncomfortably on the dresser. He wished all the talking would stop so that he could get some rest. He felt queasy and he could not understand why. Surely he had not eaten *that* much fish?

After one last attempt to persuade the trolls to sell their treasures, the stranger reluctantly left. Hildi and Thom smiled happily and waved goodbye from the door of their little dwelling in the forest. They waited until the man had disappeared into the trees and then went back inside.

They had enjoyed the visit. It had been a change to see a new face. It had been interesting to learn about the Vikings.

Strange how excited the Big Person had got over it all.

But what else could you expect from a Big Person? They *always* seemed strange to the trolls.

Grimo licked himself thoughtfully. He was not sure they had seen the last of the stranger…not sure at all…

Chapter 5

L ater that evening, when Thom and Hildi had completed their jobs for the day, they sat on their two wooden chairs by the smoking stove and thought about the visitor. Thom was unusually quiet and sat, tail in lap, chewing a piece of liquorice root. Hildi, never one to sit doing nothing, was busy repairing the patchwork cover that Grimo had torn that morning. Her stitches were tiny and careful. She peered through the candlelight, screwing up her old eyes now and then when the light flickered. It was becoming more and more of a struggle to see detail these days.

Tailo groaned in his bed. He had never had tummy ache like this before. He had not wanted any scraps at teatime and he could not understand why. In the end, he could not bear it any longer.

"Scratchen," he moaned, "I don't feel at *all* well! What's the matter with me?"

Scratchen looked over at him, scratched his left ear and did not comment. After all, hadn't he promised to get even with Tailo one of these days? It seemed to Scratchen that he had spent all his life going without enough food because greedy Tailo had always got in there first. It was time he was taught a lesson.

Tailo groaned again and clutched his swollen belly.

"Well," said Scratchen at last, "I don't suppose the Rat Poison did you any good!"

"RAT POISON!" squawked Tailo in horror. "What do you mean, Rat Poison?"

Scratchen pretended he had not heard this protest and made a big job of inspecting his claws. Tailo decided that he felt even *worse* now and panic swept over him.

"Scratchen! Scratchen! You've *GOT* to help me!" he cried and he mopped his fevered brow with one shaky, brown paw.

He understood it all now.

"I'm sorry I did not let you have any," Tailo said, without thinking properly. "I will try not to be so greedy in future!"

"Thanks very much!" replied Scratchen tartly. "I bet you *are* sorry you didn't give it to me!" and the two mice turned away from each other, Tailo now even more miserable that his apology had gone wrong as well.

Hildi looked across at Thom. He seemed wrapped up in his thoughts this evening.

"Thom?" she queried, gently.

Thom looked up and sighed. He held out one hairy hand to Hildi and she put down her sewing to take it.

"Aah, our visitori!" he offered by way of explanation. "Ve needen thingors. Visitori's moneg helpen oos."

And Thom thought once again about how he needed a new bucket and axe shaft, and how Hildi would love some new, pretty plates - a matching set even. He grasped Hildi's hand tightly. Would the money have made things easier for them after all?

Thom's thoughts began to gallop. Hildi could get a new bed cover instead of the old one she was now mending, straining her eyes in the dim candlelight to see. She could get some new clothes!

And food!

No more hard work fishing and gathering in all weathers.

Thom became excited. Perhaps they should treat these Viking things as treasure after all?

Hildi shook her head.

"Nay, nay, Thom!" she said. "Trolls hab *Troll Treasoori*, nics Viking!"

It bothered her to think that Thom was considering the value of money when they had never needed it before. The only treasure they should be interested in was the Troll Treasure. And anyway, she felt they were happy as they were and told Thom so.

Still Thom looked unsettled.

Perhaps just a small exchange of Viking coins for money would mean that Hildi's life would be that little bit easier. She would not have to work so hard at her pictures - and he needed some paint for Mistig Vorter.

So the trolls went to bed that night, uneasy and thoughtful. They had never felt like this before. Thom's troll tail twitched as his mind churned.

How involved should they get with the Big People's world?

Grimo was worried about the change in the trolls' mood. They were normally so calm and happy. There was no doubt the stranger's visit had affected them *all* - especially Tailo, of course, who weakly sipped some warm rosehip tea that Hildi had passed to him before going to bed. It soothed his stomach slightly and the vapour from it cleared his head of the muzziness he felt. He had learned a lot today. Perhaps he *should* stop being so greedy. Tailo sighed ruefully. It was going to be quite a strain, though...

The next morning, after a bad night of little sleep, Thom had made a decision. There was nothing else for it. If he did not try to use the Viking treasure to improve their difficult lives, there was no point in him having found it. And he felt strongly that it *had* to be. As he held Hildi gently in his arms the next day, he tried to get her to understand what he was doing.

"Im goingor to Bergen," he said quietly. "In Mistig Vorter boot. Ve needen moneg to helpen oos. Ve needen menig thingors - Viking Treasoori gib oos thingors, mi Hildi." Thom planted a warm kiss on Hildi's forehead. She closed her eyes tight to stop the tears.

They had never been apart before.

It would be very strange.

Bergen was such a big place with so many Big People. How would Thom cope?

A hundred worries crowded Hildi's mind.

"Oh dearig, Thom!" she sighed as her tears began to flow down her brown, wrinkled face. "Im feelen so sadli!" and she blew her large nose on the end of her little shift dress. "Kissig, kissig, Thom," she sobbed as Thom gathered her in his strong arms and reassured her.

"Oh, GIVE me a BREAK!" squeaked Tailo in great irritation from the dresser. "He's only going on a boat trip with a bit of Viking rubbish, for goodness sake!" He tut-tutted his yellow teeth and looked heavenwards.

Scratchen looked up from his bed.

"I see *you're* feeling better!" he called out, not without a note of disappointment in his voice.

"Well, really! I ask you! When we came *here*, we had a *much* longer trip on a ship than he's going to have in Misty Water boat to Bergen!" said Tailo. He really could not understand why there was all this fuss between

Hildi and Thom. His poorliness of the day before had made him feel decidedly ratty and not at all mousy this morning.

Scratchen had a feeling that Tailo was going to be rather difficult to live with for a while.

Whilst Thom was outside quickly gathering as much firewood as possible to keep Hildi warm in his absence, Hildi packed rye bread and smoked fish into a little wooden box for Thom's journey. It was not long before Thom was ready to leave.

"Im taken Viking moneg," said Thom, picking up the bag of Viking coins, which had so interested the stranger the day before. Thom did not want to take too much with him. They did not need very much money for the things they required. Besides, they had both grown rather fond of many of the items and found uses for them, so it seemed silly to get rid of any more for the time being.

Hildi, still sniffing from her earlier tears, passed Thom the food she had packed and gave him a hug.

"Gooshty borg!" she whispered hoarsely. "Gooshty luckor!"

Thom held her briefly and then, without more ado, he turned on his little troll heel and left their dwelling, striding down to the fjord with great determination.

Hildi watched him go from the doorway and then, wiping her eyes on the corner of her little shift, she went inside and closed the door quietly behind her. Grimo wound his way in and out of her hairy, brown legs and Hildi stooped to pet him.

"Urnli oos now, Grimo," she sighed. "Urnli oos."

Mistig Vorter appeared bobbing and ready for the journey ahead when Thom reached the water's edge. But today, somehow, the water of the fjord seemed dark and deep. The sky overhead had grey, threatening clouds and the mountainside was black and stony. Thom shivered as he lifted his box of food and bag of coins into the little boat. He felt the familiar prickle of fur beginning to grow at the back of his neck in response to the cold. The rope that he used to tether his boat was wet and slippery. Thom had trouble gripping it as he untied it and the firm knot would not budge.

"Ropey is strangeror todagen!" muttered Thom, puzzled.

He held the rope more firmly and jaggled the knot once more. It was as if the boat did not want to leave the shore today. Thom felt a little uncomfortable. He thought about Hildi, sitting in their home with cat and mice, nettle tea brewing and was momentarily tempted to turn back - but then he thought of her tears that morning. Had he put her through all that for nothing?

With one great tug, the knot finally gave way and the rope slid down the muddy bank and slopped into the murky, dark water. Thom quickly tucked his troll tail into the back of his green dungarees and leapt on board. He grabbed the little oars and rowed Mistig Vorter further out. It looked a fragile and delicate craft against the black water and mountains. The wind blew into Thom's face and stung his eyes. His large nose became redder than usual and he set his mouth in a hard, thin line, determined to succeed. It occurred to him, fleetingly, that it would have been much easier to have accepted the stranger's offer of money in the first place. But *then* he had not had a chance to think this thing through… and anyway, life was not supposed to be easy.

Thom's oars dip-plipped in the water as he rowed resolutely on. He quietly slipped past everything he was familiar with. Past his favourite sunning-place where he kept a few bees. The hives were dark and still.

Too cold and grey for bees today.

Thom looked up at the sky and shuddered. The dark clouds were gathering thick and fast.

On he rowed; past the occasional huge house where Big People lived; past tall, black trees and woodland; past moored boats, much bigger than his little one, until he approached the Great Waterfall's edge. The water of the fjord became turbulent and it was difficult to control Mistig Vorter. The Great Waterfall crashed down thunderingly before Thom. He steered his craft further out so that it would not be swept away and, very wobbly, the little troll got to his feet. He turned to face the rushing water and clasped both hairy hands on top of his spiky head in solemn Troll Salute. For Thom knew that somewhere behind the Great Waterfall lay the precious Troll Treasure.

"Forerver Guarderig!" Thom murmured, his eyes closed briefly.

"'Forerver Guarderig!' Thom murmured..."

His oath to guard the Troll Treasure came from the heart and Thom knew he would lay down his life to protect the trolls' True Inheritance.

A large plop of rain made Thom open his eyes once more. Then there were two more drops, then three. He had now passed the Great Waterfall and his thoughts focused on what lay before him in Bergen. He wished now that he had brought his woollen jacket with him because a cold wind was blowing and it ruffled up the troll fur on his back, as fast as it was growing.

Then the rain began to fall steadily. It spattered the surface of the fjord, making it strangely flat as far as the eye could see. Large raindrops landed on Thom's head, soaking his hair so that it plastered to him like a brown cap. More raindrops landed on his nose and broke, running down both sides of his face, and dripped off his chin. He sat, huddled in Mistig Vorter, cold and miserable.

Had this been such a good idea?

The elements seemed set against him.

Once more, Thom thought wistfully of Hildi in their snug home and he felt a pang of loneliness. This, he decided, was one of the hardest things he had ever done.

How he missed dear, little, old Hildi and her gentle ways.

The boat bobbed on further and further from his home.

The night drew in around the troll dwelling in the forest. Hildi had long since closed the red and white checked curtains in the kitchen and now she sat, Grimo in her lap, staring into the little wood fire.

Scratchen sniffed on the dresser. Tailo was napping. "Pretty quiet in here tonight!" Scratchen commented, hoping to wake Tailo for a chat. "Did you hear me, Tailo?"

Tailo just dozed.

"I said: IT'S PRETTY QUIET IN HERE TONIGHT!"

Scratchen was bored and wanted some attention. Even some Troll-Talk would have been welcome.

Grimo's ears pricked up and he cast a longing eye over to the dresser. His grey tail twitched. If it was *attention* Scratchen wanted, then he might just get it, he thought.

Tailo muttered something in his sleep and began to snore.

Scratchen started to yell.

"I've got some WONDERFUL NUT CLUSTERS and BERRY PUDDING HERE!"

Still Tailo slept. It was quite astonishing.

Maybe Tailo *was* going to be a reformed character after all, thought Scratchen. He was not too sure if he really liked that idea. He wouldn't be able to grumble about him so much now. And he did *so* enjoy doing that!

Shame...

As Hildi's eyelids drooped before the heat of the fire, a little blue boat dip-plipped its way into the harbour at Bergen. A small troll head hung down with tiredness, wet and sad.

"Sleep now, Thom," the water seemed to say as it lapped against the boat.

"Sleep now."

Chapter 6

In the cold, grey light of dawn, Thom stirred from his slumber in Mistig Vorter. For a second or two, he did not remember where he was and he sleepily stretched out a hand for Hildi. His hand did not rest on her downy hair but fell with a wooden thud against the bottom of the boat. Thom opened his eyes in surprise.

And then he woke up properly.

There was a cold, empty feeling in the pit of his stomach as he remembered how many miles away from home he was and what he was doing here.

Thom sat up and stretched, both arms in the air and fingers pointing up at the sky. He felt stiff and his shoulders ached from all the rowing of the day before. He rubbed his eyes and ruffled his spiky hair only to find that it had grown considerably in the night. Troll fur thickly covered his neck and back, where he had felt the cold.

This could be awkward, Thom thought to himself. It was never advisable to show the Big People any troll-ness. If only he had brought his woollen jacket, he would not have grown this fur, or at the very least, he would have been able to cover it up.

That was it!

He would get hold of a jacket from somewhere and cover up!

There was only one snag to this. He had none of Hildi's pictures to use for exchange and, until he sold his Viking coins, no money either. And he did not want to approach anyone looking like he did. This money business was very difficult.

Thom looked up and down the quayside where all the boats were moored. A little way down from Mistig Vorter there was a large fishing boat. It had just arrived and the crew was busy making the vessel secure. Thom kept his distance and sat watching. As luck would have it, he saw one man, warm from his exertions, remove his oilskin jacket and throw it over a mooring post on the quayside.

Thom's heart thumped.

This was just what he wanted. It would be rather big but he could shove the sleeves up.

Without hesitating, he leapt out of Mistig Vorter and, whilst the man was occupied elsewhere on the fishing boat, Thom ran towards the jacket. Snatching it from the post, he turned to dash back, but his bare, hairy foot got caught in the loop of a rope and he fell to the ground.

"Dunder-troll, Thom!" he gasped to himself as he staggered to his feet and headed back to his little boat.

Just in time!

The man was returning for his jacket before going down below for something to eat.

Thom lay low until the shouting had died down...

Hildi hummed a quiet hum as she busied herself about the kitchen. All things considered, she had not had too bad a night and everything seemed better now that it was morning again.

"Brekenfasht, Grimo!" she called to the smoky-grey ball of fur that still lay on the bed. A saucer of steaming milk and bread was placed lovingly on the kitchen floor and Grimo purred as he lapped it up. The smell of food wafted up to the mice on the dresser.

"Breakfast-time! Great!" exclaimed Tailo, forgetting for a moment his promise not to be greedy.

Scratchen looked over at him and raised one eyebrow. Tailo shuffled uncomfortably.

"After *you*, of course!" he added hurriedly and started to groom his brown coat, as if he was not really bothered whether he ate anything today or not.

Scratchen smiled to himself. This was going to be fun! Hildi passed some nuts and crumbs of bread to the mice and then went to her cupboard for some jars to bottle bilberries in. For the first time ever, Scratchen had breakfast before Tailo and he tucked in with gusto. Gobbling furiously, he polished off all the food except for a few crumbs, which he left for the other mouse. Tailo looked on anxiously.

"There!" said Scratchen, settling himself in the corner for a good scratch. "Now you know how *I've* always felt! Enjoy your breakfast!"

Tailo never said a word.

When all the noise had died down and the fisherman had stopped blaming the other members of his crew for stealing his jacket, Thom peered out of the top of Mistig Vorter, where he had been crouching.

It was time he made a move.

He wanted to get back to Hildi as soon as possible and hanging around in his boat was not going to get him anywhere. As Thom stood up, his troll tail fell behind him and he realised that he must have torn his dungarees when he fell. He tucked it in as best he could and gathered together the torn material in a sort of scrunch. He put on the jacket and shoved the sleeves up. It came down to his knees and was rather heavy.

It would have to do.

Nobody would see his tom trousers because his newly acquired jacket would cover the rip. Tightly grasping his bag of Viking coins and patting Mistig Vorter goodbye, Thom set out into the streets of Bergen.

He had not gone far when he spotted a bar where some sailors had gathered for food and drink. Cooking smells lingered outside the doorway and seemed to coax Thom in. There was much shouting and noise, the sound of mugs clanking on the tabletops and the clattering of plates as the men ate. Thom stood in the doorway and cast a wary eye around the room, in case the fisherman whose jacket he had stolen was there.

There was no sign of him.

With some relief, Thom entered. It seemed a very generous sort of place to him. From what he could see, if the Big People wanted something to drink or eat, they just asked for it and it was brought to their table.

Easy as that!

Nothing to it!

Reading from a board behind the bar, Thom asked for sausage and bread, with coffee to drink. He seated himself at a table. He had to stretch to get his elbows resting on the surface and his little, hairy legs swung from the chair, but he was comfortable enough. In due course, the food was brought to him. Thom was pleased and thanked the barman for his generosity. It was nice to know that, even in a place as big as Bergen, with people as big as this, there was warm food to be given to a hungry traveller, Thom reflected as he tucked in. He supposed it was just like him and Hildi giving the stranger refreshment the other day.

The coffee was a bit peculiar, though, not at all like Hildi's nettle or rosehip tea.

Hildi had finished her bilberry-bottling and was just about to bring in some wood for the fire when she stopped in her tracks.

Voices.

Low, gruff voices.

Big People's voices.

Grimo, Scratchen and Tailo made a dive for cover. Tailo gulped, suddenly feeling sick. The memories of the last visit were all too vivid.

Hildi worked her mouth nervously. She was all alone. Thom was not there to reassure her this time. Cautiously, she peeped through the side of the kitchen curtain and looked down the path.

A gasp caught in her throat.

Her heart started to pound.

Three Big Men were striding up towards her door.

Their faces were set in grim determination and their fists were clenched.

Leading them was the stranger who visited them before.

He did not look friendly - or lost - this time.

Hildi quickly pressed herself back against the kitchen wall. She held her breath, biting her lip and trembling.

With an enormous BANG the little door of the trolls' dwelling was smashed open and the three Big Men forced their way in. Hildi cried out in terror as the stranger from before grabbed her wrist, twisting it so that it burned in his grip. He thrust his great face in front of hers so that Hildi could smell the beer on his breath.

"Give us your treasure!" he growled.

Hildi was speechless with fright. She gulped for air and tried to cry out but no sound left her terrified lips.

Grimo, hiding, cast a swift glance up at the cuckoo clock.

Treasure? Surely not!

How did *they* know about the...

"The VIKING treasure! We want it all NOW!" yelled the stranger. He nodded at the other two men who accompanied him. "Search the house and fill the bags!"

Hildi felt sick and weak. Her hand was throbbing in the man's tight grip. The stranger smiled at her in her desperation.

"All alone, are we?" he whispered in a threatening tone, his bloodshot eyes close to Hildi's. "Tell me where every bit of the treasure is and you'll not get hurt..."

Hildi struggled feebly to free herself and began to

weep. At last she found her voice.

"Take it!" she cried and wildly waved her hand around the room to show that the Viking things were everywhere.

The Big Man laughed in her face.

"Hah! The other day, you wouldn't even *sell* me it! Now you want me to *take* it! Well, I must say, that's very generous of you!"

Hildi began to shake from head to toe. The stranger, realising that she was not going to cause him any problem, let go of her wrist and flung her to the floor. Hildi knocked her head against the wall and collapsed in a heap, her tearful eyes closed. She lay quite still.

"Why did you do that?" questioned one of the men. "We need her to tell us where it all is! For all we know, they may have stashed it away somewhere!"

"No, they haven't!" the stranger growled back. "I told you, they didn't have any idea of its value. It wouldn't occur to them to hide it! Now get on with it!"

The Big Men ransacked the little house. The silver crosses, Thor's hammer on the gold chain, the pendants, brooches, bronze keys and neck rings, the knives, beakers, bowls, the spear heads, axe-head and swords - all went into the Big Men's sacks.

Even Hildi's precious glass beads were snatched from around her neck, as she lay slumped on the floor.

The only items missed were the Vendel helmet,

covered as it was with a trailing plant, and the Wodan figurine on top of the dresser.

After five minutes of complete madness, the three Big Men left the little house in the forest. The door was left open, hanging on only one hinge. The table was over-turned and the chairs lay strewn about the floor. Hildi's pictures lay tattered and torn. Her little pans and troll pots were emptied from the cupboards and her herbs were scattered over the kitchen. The bed was turned upside down, the patchwork quilt ripped in the Big Men's frenzy.

The wind whistled through the open door and made the red and white checked curtains flap. Outside, the rain began once more.

Thom finished his tasty meal and wiped his mouth on the back of his hand. Now he must get down to some business, he thought. As he stood to leave, the barman appeared at his side.

"Did you enjoy your meal?" he questioned.

"Oh, yes!" replied Thom in all innocence. "Very tasty, thank you. But now I must say 'Goodbye' and be on my way!"

The barman's smile vanished.

"Haven't you forgotten something?" he snarled.

Thom was concerned for a moment and looked about him.

"No," he said. "I've got everything I came in with, thank you!"

"But you shouldn't have *everything*, should you?" the barman said, raising his voice a little. "You should have less *MONEY* now, because you should have paid for the food!"

Thom suddenly felt nervous. He had no money. He did not understand money and had not understood this system of *buying* food. He took a step towards the door.

In a flash, the barman had hold of the collar of his jacket and hitched him off the ground.

"Where's my money?" he demanded.

Everyone in the bar turned round to look.

And then to laugh...

For, as Thom dangled in the air, his jacket revealed the tear in his dungarees and his troll tail had fallen out.

"Look at his TAIL!" one person shouted.

"He's so HAIRY!" shouted another.

"And he's even got HAIRY FEET!" called out a third. "What are you, little man, a TROLL or something?"

And there was a great jeering and noise.

Thom thought quickly. He was desperate. His only thought was to escape from this awful situation as quickly as possible.

"Let me down! Let me down, I'll pay!" he shouted

as loudly as he could above the rest of the din.

The barman dropped him to his feet and towered menacingly over him.

Thom, with shaking fingers, fumbled in the pockets of the stolen jacket he was wearing and drew out the bag of Viking coins. He flung some onto the table in front of the barman's astonished face.

The room fell silent.

The barman picked up one of the coins and bit it, testing it for the real thing.

All of a sudden, he made a lunge for the coins that lay scattered on the tabletop. Others around him did the same. They had recognised the coins for what they really were. In an instant, the silence was broken and everyone in the bar dived for the table.

Thom took his chance and fled but some of the Big Men made chase. On and on through the streets of Bergen he ran, his breath coming out in great panting gasps. Gradually, the noise of feet behind him disappeared and he slowed down.

The harbour lay before him.

At the side of Mistig Vorter at last, thinking he was safe from being followed, Thom flung the remaining coins and bag into the depths of the fjord.

He had a very uneasy feeling inside.

All was not well.

Thom shakily removed the fisherman's jacket and

left it on the quayside for the man to find once more. He climbed into his little boat and grabbed hold of the oars.

This had not been a good trip. It was time he was home. He felt Hildi needed him.

As Mistig Vorter made its way through the water, Thom shuddered. He was not sure why...

Surely that was not the shadow of a boat behind him?

Chapter 7

C ome on, Scratchen! Help me!" Tailo squeaked from Hildi and Thom's bedroom, as he tried to pull the torn patchwork cover into the kitchen. "Hildi will not survive the wind and cold unless we cover her up!"

"What? I never thought of that!" yelped Scratchen scurrying to Tailo's aid.

It was quite true. The wind howled through the broken kitchen door and the rain was slanting down onto the floor. Hildi still lay slumped in shock, her wispy, white hair being blown back from her face and her skin chilled.

The two mice each grabbed a corner of the cover in their teeth and scrabbled on the floor to get a grip to pull against. Grimo saw their concern and jumped down from his hiding- place to help.

"OH, NO!" yelled Tailo. "That's ALL we need! THAT CAT is going to eat us now! RUN FOR IT!" And the two mice fled in panic.

When they looked behind them though, Scratchen and Tailo were amazed to see that Grimo was trying to help them. He had gone to the far side of the cover and was pushing it with his nose and front paws.

The two mice cautiously returned to their corners and began to tug again. Little by little, the cover slid across the cold floor to where Hildi lay. Grimo then joined Tailo and Scratchen at the top end of the cover and they all pulled together until it rested over Hildi's shoulders.

The animals sat down in a panting heap beside her. This was something they had never done before...

...They had *all* worked *together* to help the little troll who always did so much for them.

They looked at each other in surprise.

They had a curious *warm* feeling in their tummies, despite the chill wind.

It felt good.

Grimo looked at Hildi. Her face still seemed too cold. He gently walked up her slumped body and settled himself down in a warming, furry heap on the top of her head.

Tailo and Scratchen saw this.

"Well, what do you think of that!" exclaimed Tailo in surprise. "THAT CAT is more useful than we thought! He makes a brilliant hat!"

"And if *he* can make himself into a hat, we can make ourselves into ear muffs!" laughed Scratchen and, so saying, he scampered up Hildi's face and curled into a tight ball over one ear. Tailo, not to be left out of all this thoughtfulness, warmed the other ear.

And so it was that when Thom finally reached his little dwelling in the forest, his heart thumping with fear for Hildi's safety, he found just inside the broken-down door, his beloved soul mate kept safe from the chilling rain and biting wind.

"Hildi! Mi dearig, lovelor Hildi!" Thom cried as he scooped her up in his strong arms to cradle her sweet, old head against his chest. The animals fell from her in a disgruntled heap onto the kitchen floor. Hot tears ran down Thom's face and fell onto Hildi's cheeks and closed eyelids.

Thom carried her gently to their bed, much disturbed by the mess the Big Men had left. As he stroked Hildi's face and warmed her frail, brown hands in his, she began to murmur - and then to open her eyes.

Thom gasped with relief.

He told Hildi to lie still as, shakily, he got some special Troll-Cherry Wine from the cupboard, kept for warming them on bitter, winter nights. As Hildi came round, she told Thom what had happened in his absence and they held each other and sobbed until they felt strong again.

"Viking Treasoori nics gooshty foor trolls!" Thom

said quietly to Hildi. "Biggy Menor so badli! Moneg mekken Biggy Menor badli!"

"Moneg is badli!" Hildi said gravely, knowing now that she was right in her feelings that trolls had no use for money. It only caused trouble.

The two trolls smiled and sighed. At least now, with the Viking treasure stolen and the rest of the Viking coins at the bottom of the fjord, they could relax and forget about the whole thing.

It was a great relief.

Silently, as the grey water lapped the bank, a strange, large boat slipped beside Mistig Vorter and was made secure. The black craft had BERGEN painted on the side.

Whilst Hildi lay resting, Thom set to and tidied their home. Propping up the door in the frame to fix later, he told Hildi about how the animals saved her life by keeping her warm. They had all been given special hugs, which Tailo found rather embarrassing, and some special food bits, which they all gobbled with great pleasure.

Scratchen and the trolls were pleased to see Tailo keep to his share. He really was trying hard to be a good mouse.

The herbs were swept up; pots and pans were put back in the cupboard; Hildi's strewn pictures were sorted and put away, and the bed was tidied.

"Hah!" exclaimed Thom. "Biggy Menor leftig tvo Viking thingors!"

Hildi looked at him in surprise. She thought that the Big Men had taken *all* the Viking objects. But no, the Vendel helmet was still there on the windowsill, hidden by the plant.

And there, fallen over and so difficult to see, at the top of the dresser was the statue of Wodan.

Hildi shuddered. It did not feel good to see something left.

A black and white tracker dog jumped out of the boat from Bergen and wagged its tail expectantly. Its sniffing nose snuffled this way and that in the mud around Mistig Vorter.

"Which way did he go, blast him? I hope we've not followed him all the way from Bergen for nothing!" growled Tromsvag, his bushy eyebrows knitting together in a dark scowl. He kicked at the dog and snarled, "Find the troll! Do you hear me? Find the troll, quickly!"

"Keep your voice down, Tromsvag!" Flossik hissed. "If he *is* around here, we don't want him to know we have landed - especially if he has sloped off to his Viking treasure hideout!" And he drew his scarf up over his mouth and nose. His weasely eyes peered out above it, searching for a sign of Thom.

Tromsvag grabbed the dog by the scruff of its neck and roughly shoved it into Mistig Vorter. Drools of spit fell from the dog's curled lips as it picked up the strong smell of fish from the bottom of the boat. It sniffed around the seat and the little, sturdy oars until it was sure of Thom's troll-scent. Then, the burly Tromsvag hoisted the dog out of Mistig Vorter and set it after the quarry. Flossik smiled a thin smile under his scarf as he saw their dog bound off along a hardly noticeable path, through the forest.

"Let's go!"

Thom drove the last screw into the hinge of the kitchen door and, with sighs of relief from one and all, he shut it against the cold wind outside.

"Doori fixig, Hildi!" he called through to Hildi who

was still resting.

"Yo, yo! Thanken, thanken!" Hildi replied with a smile as she snuggled down into the warmth of her bed. It was so good to have Thom back with her.

She felt safe once more.

Grimo had finally finished grooming himself and felt happy and contented. The two mice were resting on the dresser, squeaking a little as they shuffled around to get comfortable. Grimo cast a glance up at them. Making friends with those two was all very well - in an hour of need - but it was going to reduce the fun a bit. How could you chase and eat your friends?

Big mistake!

Grimo swished his tail slightly, his contentment faltering for a moment, and then he jumped up to look out of the kitchen window. There was nothing for it, he decided, he would have to go out to play catch with some forest-mice instead.

Thom laughed as he let Grimo out through the door. It was so typical of a cat to want to go out the minute the door was fixed and shut, instead of going when it had been hanging open! Grimo ignored him and set off along the forest path.

And immediately wished he had not.

What he saw ahead of him made him screech with fright!

His fur stood up on end and his claws shot out. His

ears flattened.

DOG!

Grimo's eyes widened in horror as the dog advanced. Its tongue lolled out between its huge fangs and it slobbered from the jowls. The bloodshot eyes spotted Grimo and it bounded towards him, barking furiously. Dog smell came with it.

With a fearful H-O-W-L, Grimo fled back up the path, with the frantic dog in hot pursuit.

"With a fearful H-O-W-L, Grimo fled..."

"Come back, you stupid hound!" shouted Tromsvag forgetting once more to be quiet, in his fury at the distracted dog.

"Shut up, you fool!" spat Flossik as he ran after the animals. "Do you want to let the troll know we are coming? Now, catch the dratted dog before he loses the trail altogether and hurry!"

Flossik sped up the path, Tromsvag lumbering behind.

Grimo, still screeching in terror, reached the trolls' dwelling and shot through a hole into the shed at the side. The dog was left whining and sniffing around the opening, scrabbling with his great paws to reach him.

The two Big Men had almost caught up with their dog when suddenly they stopped in their tracks, as they saw the little home.

"Well, well!" smirked Flossik. "The dog was not so stupidly out of control after all! The troll's cat has led us right to him!"

And it was indeed true.

Grimo, in his panic and innocence, had unwittingly brought Hildi and Thom yet more trouble.

The barking of the dog sent Tailo and Scratchen scurrying further up the dresser, squeaking madly - all eyes and whiskers - and Hildi gripped Thom in terror.

The door, mended but not bolted, was flung open, and there on the threshold stood Flossik and the huge Tromsvag. Their hair was wild with the wind and their eyes shone with greed. Flossik ran his tongue over his teeth and favoured the two terrified trolls with a cunning, slow smile. Tromsvag glowered over Flossik's shoulder, his black beard flecked with spit from running up the path.

"So, my little friend," Flossik smirked, menacingly, "this is where you hide out! We've come a long way to talk to you!" and he took two steps into the kitchen. Tromsvag followed.

Hildi and Thom were speechless.

"Aren't you going to invite us in?" Flossik continued, taking hold of a little chair and putting one boot up on it.

"It looks like you already *are* in!" Thom said quietly, his heart pounding as he held Hildi tightly against him.

"Tut, tut!" smiled Flossik, half turning to Tromsvag and adding, "not very friendly, are they?"

"What do you want?" questioned Thom through gritted teeth. "We have nothing to interest Big People here."

"Aah, not so, little troll, not so!" Flossik shook his head. He leaned forward towards Thom, his smile gone. "You have Viking money- and WE WANT IT!"

"No, no!" replied Thom, his voice shaking. "We

have none!"

Flossik snapped his fingers together at Tromsvag. The dog was brought in from outside. On seeing the strange trolls, it barked and then began to growl. Its teeth were bared and its bloodshot eyes were popping and staring as it strained against Tromsvag's grip.

Hildi let out a tiny moan of fear and began to shake.

"Now, now, Troll! Don't lie to me!" Flossik snarled, dog-like himself. "We *KNOW* you have Viking gold - we saw you throwing it about in the café in Bergen!"

Thom swallowed even though his mouth was dry.

Flossik kicked over the chair he had been resting on and took one stride over to the quaking trolls. He grabbed some of Thom's spiky hair in his grimy fist and tilted Thom's head backwards.

"TELL ME WHERE IT IS!" he yelled.

There was mad squeaking from above as the two mice frantically covered their ears. They were on the top shelf of the dresser and still did not feel safe.

The Wodan figure was watching.

It was beginning to shake.

Tailo was *sure* he had not knocked it.

It was as though the statue was sensing the violence and tension in the room.

Absorbing it...

Using it...

Flossik did not take his eyes off Thom's face and so

did not notice. All he wanted was money.

"WELL?" he bellowed.

Thom stammered his reply. "I - I - I threw the rest away!"

Flossik banged the back of Thom's head against the wall. The dog tried to lunge forwards.

"My dog doesn't believe you!" hissed the Big Man in Thom's frightened face.

Hildi found her voice. "It's true! The Viking money was *trouble* for us - we did not want it any more. Thom threw it into the fjord!"

"PAH!" spat Flossik and let go of Thom's hair. He turned to Tromsvag. "Let the dog guard them whilst we search the place. It must be hidden *somewhere!*"

The Big Men roughly pushed past Hildi and Thom, whilst the fierce dog stood its ground in front of them.

The men were too big for the trolls' home. They knocked against things and sent them crashing to the floor.

And then it happened.

It made Thom break out in a sweat of fear and a wash of sickness.

Tromsvag did it.

He pushed in front of Flossik, brushing against the cuckoo clock on the wall. His jacket shoulder caught on the clock catch, which, although mended, still stuck out slightly.

The clock face swung open.

There at Flossik's feet lay the hidden Troll Map.

Thom gasped.

All of every troll's True Inheritance lay within Flossik's grasp.

The Troll Treasure.

Flossik stopped in his tracks. He stooped to pick up the ancient map and a satisfied smile crept over his face.

"Well, well!" he breathed. "What have we here?" Thom took a step forwards, despite the growling dog.

"Please," he began, "that does not concern you - let me have it back!"

"What?" questioned Flossik, holding the tatty piece of paper above Thom's head, just out of his reach. "This?" He lowered it slowly down, only to snatch it back into his grimy fist as Thom shot out his hand for it.

Tromsvag came to look at the map.

"What is it?" he asked Flossik.

"Why - it's a map of course!" came the reply. "The little fool troll has thought to trick us by *hiding* his Viking gold away and telling us he has thrown it into the fjord!"

Tromsvag began to smile, and then to chuckle, and then to laugh.

The two Big Men threw back their heads and roared.

"WE HAVE IT!" Tromsvag shouted.

"PLEASE!" begged Thom above the noise. "I'll do ANYTHING! That is NOT Viking money! You don't understand what you HAVE!"

The Big Men did not even look at him. They yanked the collar of the dog, which was now leaping about with excitement and wagging his tail furiously, and left the trolls' home.

The two trolls stared down the path, still shaking, watching them go.

Hildi and Thom turned to look at each other in dismay.

This meant Big Trouble.

Chapter 8

As the Big Men hurried away, Hildi covered her little, tired face with her hands and started to cry. Great tears rolled down her cheeks and into the cracks between her fingers.

"Dee Troll Treasoori! Oh, Thom, Thom!" she sobbed.

Thom knew how she felt. This was sickening. It was every troll's duty to protect the Troll Treasure so that it could be saved for a time of great need. A time when *all* trolls were threatened. The whole of the troll species depended on it.

And now it could be in the Big Men's hands.

Thom knew he could not let this happen.

He was responsible for all this mess. He must sort it out.

"Forerver Guarderig", the Trolls' Motto, was not said easily and was not lightly meant. Thom's mouth set in a determined line. He must act upon his solemn vow.

"Im goingor guarderig Troll Treasoori!" he said in a grim voice.

Tailo and Scratchen peeped down from their snug

bed. Guarding the Troll Treasure? They looked at each other in surprise.

This was very brave.

This was very noble.

This was very dangerous.

Tailo shook his furry, black head…

This was *very* stupid.

Hildi looked tearfully at her beloved partner. She did not say a word. She knew as well as Thom how important troll vows were. She knew Thom had no other choice but to follow the Big Men to the secret place behind the Great Waterfall. She knew that *any* troll in his position would protect the Troll Treasure with his life.

Hildi just prayed Thom would not have to do so.

Thom reached for his woollen jacket and then gave Hildi a silent embrace. Neither of them could speak. It was just as Thom was turning for the door that he heard the mice squeaking. Tailo and Scratchen set up a fearful racket. They had scampered up to the top of the dresser and were clambering all over the forgotten figurine of Wodan.

"Take this, Thom!" screeched Scratchen, furiously scratching his tummy in agitation.

"Yes!" yelled Tailo, as loudly as a mouse can yell. "Take it! They may settle for having this, instead of the map!"

The figurine began to throb. Its vibrations shivered through the mice as they held on round its neck. Thom hesitated, doubtful at the idea of the Big Men settling for *anything* less than great wealth.

"And the h-h-helmet!" squealed Scratchen, his voice shaking with the figurine's movement.

Thom glanced at the Vendel helmet on the windowsill, still covered in plant... After all, it had made him feel warrior-like that day when he tried it on. He looked to Hildi for agreement and saw her nod her head feverishly. The first stranger had specially asked about Vendel helmets so they *must* be worth *something* to these Big People.

Thom grabbed the plant from inside the helmet without delay and threw it to the floor. He slammed the Viking helmet on his head. He did not look ridiculous to the mice this time. Thom turned towards the figure of Wodan, as if waiting for a reaction.

"F-f-for goodn-n-ness sake, T-T-Thom!" chattered Tailo's teeth through the statue's frenzied shaking, "T-t-take the dratted thing w-w-with you! W-w-we don't w-w-want it, d-d-do we?" and Wodan shook so violently that, despite the mice desperately clinging to it, the figurine fell from the top shelf of the dresser right into Thom's outstretched hands.

It seemed like a good idea. The Big Men might accept the figure and helmet in exchange for the map -

or the Troll Treasure itself, if they ever got that far.

Heaven forbid!

But time was ticking on. He must be on his way. Thom must prove himself.

Wodan lay still in his grasp...as if waiting...

Hildi bade farewell to a very different Thom.

A stronger, braver Thom. A troll filled with purpose and a determination to see the job through.

An unsmiling Thom.

A Warrior Troll.

Hildi forgot her fear. She felt very proud.

Thom had studied the Troll Treasure map, wonderingly, many times and, as a consequence, knew it well. He took great troll strides and leaps down to the fjord edge and to his trusty boat, Mistig Vorter. There were lines and footprints in the mud where the Big Men's craft had been. There were also paw marks.

Thom shuddered when he thought of the dog.

He jumped into his boat and began to row as quickly as he could. The two long journeys to Bergen and back had tired him though, and his arms ached as he forced them to work the oars. He rowed past trees and woodland, other moored boats and odd houses, just as before. There was no sign of the Bergen boat ahead. The Big Men had got a good start on him.

"Fastli! Fastli, Mistig Vorter!" Thom urged his tiny boat as the sweat broke out on his forehead.

The figurine lay in his lap. Wodan's great, piercing eyes were staring at the grey sky overhead. The ravens at his hoofed feet looked glossy and black, their hooked beaks still clamped on the meat. The wolves still gazed up at Wodan, lean, hungry and obedient.

Thom rowed and rowed. He thought of nothing but his mission. He allowed no frightening thoughts to enter his mind. His teeth were clamped hard together and his eyes strained to see the first sign of the Big Men ahead.

The water became whirling and difficult as Thom approached the Great Waterfall. It churned and swirled, making it hard for him to steer Mistig Vorter. The thundering increased as Thom edged nearer and nearer. He fought to control the little boat and pushed hard against the current. It rose and fell alarmingly. It was impossible to stand this near to the Great Waterfall and repeat his solemn vow so, still sitting, he shouted over the crashing of the water:

"FORERVER GUARDERIG!"

The water splashed in Thom's face and the noise of the cascade made his shout seem like a whisper. Thom screwed his eyes up to peer through the spray.

Was the opening to the Great Cave visible?

Was that the Big Men's boat, safely secured at the bank under the Great Waterfall?

Yes! They had reached the back of the falls!

Thom knew he must hurry. It was pointless for a small troll like him, in a small boat like this, to approach the Great Waterfall directly. He must veer to the side and run along the bank to the Great Cave's opening.

Thom changed course and was immediately carried away by the current.

Tromsvag was beginning to feel a little uncomfortable. The air in the low-roofed passages was stale and they appeared to be going deeper and deeper into the earth.

"Wait, Flossik!" he panted, his great frame jammed up against the sides of the narrow passage. "I can't breathe too well. I don't like this place!"

"Bah!" spat Flossik. "What's the matter with you? Don't you want to be rich? If you fuss like this, we'll *never* get to the Viking treasure that little worm has hidden down here!" He viciously kicked out at their dog to send him ahead of them. The dog ran on, nose down.

Tromsvag looked about him. It had been all right at first. The cave behind the waterfall had been large and airy. They had consulted the tatty map and had decided which passageway to follow. They had started without any difficulty. The passage had been unlit at first, it was true, but at least there had been enough room for him to move along with relative ease. After the left turn downwards, things had got a bit tight - and cold too.

There were lamps on these deep passage walls. They burned gently with a curious blue glow, which made everything look strange. Natural cave gas was being used in a thin stream, through tiny, drilled holes in the walls of the passage. Occasionally, they flickered as the gas supply varied, causing Tromsvag to hold his breath, frightened that they might go out altogether and leave him in utter blackness. His worry, together with the close confines of his surroundings, made the Big Man out of breath.

"Hurry up, you great oaf!" hissed Flossik. "The dog has gone ahead of us - I don't want to lose him!" And, bending low, he struggled on, stopping only to look at the map.

Onwards and downwards, shivering with cold.

Taking first one passage, then the next...

Deeper into the earth.

Thom had reached the bank at last and had run like the wind along the muddy, slippery ground. His helmet, amazingly, stayed securely on his head and he clutched the statue, hoping against hope that he would not be too late.

He must reach the Troll Treasure quickly.

He remembered which passage to choose when he reached the Great Cave and hurled himself down it, his troll feet firm and sure. This was easy territory for him.

The troll lights seemed to welcome Thom. He was not unnerved by the blue glow. These passages felt comfortable to him; just the right height and width. He did not feel at all unsure of himself. Fur began to grow thickly on his troll body, keeping him warm and he had no difficulty remembering the route. There was to be no stopping him now.

Wodan throbbed gently in Thom's grip.

The little troll was too intent on his purpose to notice.

The statue was becoming warm.

Thom ran on and on through the passages, never hesitating.

Wodan was absorbing the energy of Thom's urgency.

"You know what *I* think?" Flossik smiled through the dim, blue glow of the lamps at his friend.

"W - w - what?" shivered Tromsvag, his teeth chattering with the cold. He was not very interested. He wanted to get out of this confusing maze.

"*I* think that we are onto *something big*!" Flossik replied, not in the slightest bit concerned about his friend's obvious discomfort. "These passages are not natural; they have been carved into the rock. You can't tell me that the puny troll has been able to do this! And the lamps! It must have taken a whole *army* of trolls to set this lot up!"

Tromsvag nodded. It certainly seemed curious.

"Didn't that troll shout: 'You don't understand what you have!'?" Flossik continued, with a crafty smile on his face.

Tromsvag could not remember.

He was not sure that he cared at this stage.

"*I* think we are about to understand what we have rather *well*," smirked Flossik nastily, "and pretty soon, too!"

Thom was now so close to the Big Men that he heard Flossik's cackle of laughter echoing through the passages. He gripped the figurine tighter, willing his plan to work. The Big Men would *have* to take this and the Vendel helmet, instead of the Troll Treasure.

They *must*!

Wodan glowed hotly in Thom's hand; his power and strength was growing all the time.

Thom did not feel it.

Without warning, the narrow passage opened up before Flossik and Tromsvag. They shouted and slapped each other on the back, relieved to have reached their goal. The tracker dog yelped in pleasure at the Big Men's obvious happiness and, eager for a well-deserved fuss, bounded backwards and forwards in a mad dance. They took no notice. The noise of their rejoicing echoed and reverberated, charging the air with excitement.

Thom heard it and grimaced.

Wodan felt the charged air and absorbed it...

The cavern was filled with stalagmites and stalactites. They shone in a hundred colours because the lamps in this place were varied. The light from them played on the Big Men's forms and cast huge shadows on the dripping walls.

Suddenly, Flossik raised his hand for silence. The dog, afraid of being struck, quietened immediately and sank to the floor, whining. Tromsvag looked at Flossik, not knowing the next move.

At the far side of the cavern was a sealed, bolted door. It was wooden and sturdy. The lamps at either side of it lit up the inscription upon it:

> "AAH, TIMES MUST BE BAD, MY LITTLE TROLL
> FOR YOU TO VENTURE HERE,
> GREAT NEED IS YOURS –
> FOR ALL OUR SAKES
> KEEP TROLL INHERITANCE DEAR."

"Troll Inheritance, eh?" read Flossik aloud.

"What's that then?" questioned Tromsvag. He did not read much and big words confused him greatly. Poetry had never been one of his interests and he was not in the mood for riddles just now.

"Inheritance means something that is passed down from generation to generation!" Flossik hissed, impatiently. "Wealth! Riches! Money! Jewels, perhaps!" he added, smiling his best, calculating smile. He rattled at the bolts, which held the door securely. They were old and rusty and had seized up over the many years of dampness in the cavern.

"Tromsvag, FORCE IT!" commanded Flossik.

Tromsvag started taking several hulking steps backwards, ready to rush at the door.

Flossik held his breath, hardly able to contain his greedy excitement.

The dog backed away, ears flattened, waiting for the crash and splintering of breaking wood.

"NO!" thundered Thom from the shadows. "YOU WILL NOT DO THIS!"

Gripping the figurine tightly for courage, his Vendel helmet squarely on his head, Thom flung himself across the wooden door, his arms and legs outstretched.

He felt brave and wild.

"Out of the way, you little fool!" blasted Flossik, angry at this last minute interruption to his plans.

"NEVER!"

"Then we'll have to MAKE you!" Flossik growled, baring his teeth like a mad dog. "Tromsvag! CARRY ON!"

Tromsvag put his head down ready to charge the door once more.

"WAIT!" yelled Thom. "HEAR WHAT I HAVE TO OFFER!"

Flossik was suddenly amused. It really was quite comical to see such a small man as *this*, troll-tail dangling between his legs, trying to stand up to the likes of *them*. He held up his hand to stall Tromsvag.

"Well, Troll, what *have* you got to offer us? A mere trifle, no doubt!" Flossik sneered and he took two menacing steps towards Thom.

Very slowly, not taking his eyes off the Big Man, Thom placed the statue of Wodan on the damp floor of the cavern.

It stood firmly in front of Flossik and Tromsvag and stared at them.

The tracker dog whimpered and backed off further into the shadows.

"THIS?" shouted Flossik, staring in disbelief at the figurine. "You must think I'm easily satisfied, Troll! I don't want this tin-pot toy! I don't think you understand what sort of trouble you are in!"

The Big Man raised his fist to strike the little troll.

Thom raised his hand to protect himself from the blow.

A split second before the blow fell, Thom realised that the hand he had raised was not hairy like his other. He had grown fur all over his body in the cold air of these passages, but not on the hand that had held Wodan.

Why was the statue so warm?

And then the blow struck home.

Thom slunk down the sturdy, wooden door to the floor.

Chapter 9

Then it happened.

The terrible, tremendous happening.

The full fury and wrath of Wodan was upon them!

The statue, so respected by the trolls because they sensed its powers, became fully charged and vital. The violence, twice witnessed in the trolls' home had been absorbed. Thom's urgent dash to save the Troll Treasure had given the statue a throbbing energy. The excitement in the cavern had been felt, along with Thom's tension.

And now, these two ignorant men had not understood Wodan.

They had rejected the statue as worthless.

They should not have underestimated Wodan's strength.

A rumbling growl grew to a great roar and filled the cavern, echoing round it, carrying on down the passages to the very heart of the underworld. The lamps were snuffed out in the sudden rush of cold air that swirled around Flossik and Tromsvag. They clung to each other in fear, gulping and gasping, their eyes wide and terrified. All thoughts of poor Thom were gone from their minds. The Troll Treasure would have to wait.

And from the floor where the statue stood, there began to glow a light.

Red - through to orange - to yellow - and to white. A dazzling, startling, white, piercing light, growing from a speck to a pulsing cloud.

Flossik and Tromsvag shouted out in fright and pain as the light shot into their eyes, almost blinding them. Their screams gave the final charge needed.

There was a deafening CRASH!... a thundering of falling rock and...

WODAN stood before them!

The Viking god of War.

The Viking god of Wisdom.

The Master of Runic Magic and Sorcerers.

Wodan the Shape-Changer.

There he stood in all his glory before the two terrified men. They cowered and whimpered, clinging to each other, weak and broken. They stared, horrified, at the beastly head with its wild, shining eyes and hooked beak. The matted, black hair fell from his great head over his shoulders and chest to his waist. He tossed his mane back and laughed a menacing, animal laugh.

"BEHOLD WODAN!" the beast roared at Flossik and Tromsvag.

At this, the two men fell onto their knees, shaking and horrified.

Wodan stamped his hoofed feet in impatience. The

energy from within was bursting for release. He raised the muscular arm that carried his Viking spear and brought it crashing down onto the rocks where he stood.

Two pairs of yellow eyes appeared at either side of the Viking god, lurking, slanted and evil. As Flossik and Tromsvag stared, transfixed, two lean and hungry wolves took form in the white haze around Wodan. They bared their yellow, fanged teeth at the men in front of their master and growled, deep-throated and low. With ears flattened back and with hackles raised, the wolves approached the gibbering men who were once so bold.

"NO!" screamed Flossik in panic. His scream frightened Tromsvag. He had never known Flossik to be out of control and not in charge of a situation. Tromsvag covered his head and huddled on the ground in a miserable heap. He screwed his eyes tight shut and tried to stop the blubbering of his lips.

Wodan raised his great spear once more and the wolves froze in their steps.

"W - w - what do you want from us?" stammered Flossik at last, wringing his hands in despair. He glanced at the slumped form of Thom by the wooden door. "T - take the troll! You can do what you like with *him*..."

Wodan made no reply. It had not been Thom who had offended him. He raised his other hand in the air and swirled it around twice.

Down flew two huge, fearsome ravens with blooded

meat dripping from their shining beaks.

"Down flew two huge, fearsome ravens with bloodied meat dripping from their shining beaks..."

They swooped around Wodan's great beastly head and then flew through the cavern, turning quickly, to dive at the crouched men. Flossik and Tromsvag felt the rush of stinking air and the brush of their powerful wings on their bent backs.

"PLEASE!" begged Tromsvag, shuddering with huge sobs. "Let us go!"

The great black ravens swooped again, their sharp claws scratching and hooking at the men's clothes. Tromsvag's face squashed right against the rock bed of the cavern.

"Money! Is it money you want?" questioned Flossik, wrongly assuming that he could buy his way out of *any* sort of trouble.

Wodan became furious at this and his great roar filled the cavern once more. In a flash of brilliant white he vanished. The air hung heavy with his animal smell though and Flossik and Tromsvag were far from relieved at his sudden disappearance.

"What now, Flossik?" Tromsvag asked shakily. The wolves were still frozen and the ravens were perching high up in the rock face. The two men did not dare move. They could not risk attack by Wodan's servants.

"I don't know..." whispered Flossik. His face was taut with fear and he could not take his eyes off the wolves.

Tromsvag dared to lift his face from the rock to look around him.

A curious sound filled the air.

"SSSSSSS!"

And then a hissing voice spoke to the men.

"You are in the pressssence of Wodan the SSSShape-Changer!"

The men gasped and, without thinking of the wolves

or ravens now, leapt to their feet, for the cavern was filled with snakes.

A hideous, seething mass of snakes.

They writhed over the floor and slithered over Flossik and Tromsvag's feet. In seconds, the two men were knee deep in them. Flossik could stand it no longer. With a yell of absolute terror he jumped at Tromsvag and attempted to climb up the bigger man, hoping to escape the flicking tongues and gliding bodies. Tromsvag was not ready for this and lost his balance. His heavy boots slipped and collapsed under him. The two men landed amongst the very creatures they wanted to avoid and the snakes lost no time in sliding all over them.

"Aaagh!" spluttered Tromsvag. "I can't breathe!"

"You fool!" spat Flossik. "Why didn't you hold me?"

"I couldn't! I didn't expect you to jump at me like that!" replied Tromsvag, twisting and turning in an attempt to get a secure footing to stand up.

One enormous python started to edge its way forwards. The two men stared at it and gulped. A long, black snake-tongue slicked in and out, smelling them, getting closer... and closer...

Just when Tromsvag was sure that it would strike, he heard Flossik trying to make another deal with Wodan. It alarmed him even more.

"Take this bumbling fool, Tromsvag!" Flossik was

shouting into the depths of the cavern. "He will do whatever you ask! But spare me! PLEASE!"

Tromsvag was not at all happy with this. It had been one thing to offer Wodan, the troll, and it was certainly a good idea to offer money to appease the Viking god - but to hand *him* over was quite a different matter! Tromsvag turned to Flossik to protest at this lack of loyalty when -

- the snakes suddenly vanished.

The men looked at each other, wondering what was coming next.

Cobwebs.

A thin silver film began to float through the air. It swirled like the morning mist around the men and settled around their ankles.

"What's this?" asked Flossik, lifting one foot but finding it stuck tightly to his other.

"Oh, no! Not cobwebs!" cried Tromsvag, in despair. "If these are the cobwebs, how big are the spiders going to be?" And he looked wildly around him, his eyes searching the nooks and crannies of the cavern.

Flossik tried again.

"Take him! Take Tromsvag - do what you will with

him! But let me go free!"

At these words, Tromsvag did his best to lunge at Flossik but, to his dismay, he found the cobwebs were creeping up their bodies. The men struggled and stretched their arms in the air to keep their hands free.

Was that a shadow of a spider lurking over there?

Flossik watched it warily.

Something was definitely moving in the darkness...

Didn't spiders wrap up their prey before they SUCKED THE BLOOD OUT?

Tromsvag was forgetting his fright because of his anger with Flossik. This was all Flossik's fault. It had been *Flossik's* idea to follow the troll home to steal the treasure *and* his idea to follow the troll's map. And now Flossik was trying to get rid of *him*! After all the help he had given him!

At the far side of the cavern, a dark shape sat up and raised an arm to rub its head.

Flossik could not think straight. He was bewildered and confused with fear.

"Please take away the spider!" he begged, his voice sounding wheedling and thin.

Thom, coming round in the darkness, heard Flossik's voice. He rubbed his head where it hurt once more...

"IT'S THERE!" screamed Flossik, unable to contain himself. "THERE'S A SPIDER OVER THERE!"

A rumbling laugh bellowed through the cavern. And then it stopped abruptly.

"ENOUGH!" the voice of Wodan commanded.

Tromsvag and Flossik waited.

By the wooden door, still guarding the treasure, Spider-Thom waited. He was not at all keen to show himself. Being mistaken for a spider was his best weapon against these men.

Then knives and swords came curling through the air.

Tromsvag saw his chance. Nobody called *him* a bumbling fool and got away with it! He grabbed a knife and cut through the cobwebs that entangled him. He turned in a rage against Flossik.

"NO!" screeched Flossik, in panic, and he plucked a Viking sword from the air for himself.

The two men stood apart in the great, dark cavern and faced each other. They were filled with a hatred they had never felt before.

"SO BE IT!" Wodan's voice rang out. "I have turned you against each other! And so it shall ALWAYS be!"

The men barely listened, so great was their fury. But Thom heard…

"You shall be forever locked in deadly combat with each other!" Wodan continued. "You shall NEVER escape these passages. You will fight with each other forever more. "For I am Wodan! I turn man against man!"

There was a great flash of light. It filled the cavern and showed up Thom, still crouching, spider-like by the troll door.

"YOU, TROLL!" Wodan bellowed.

Thom started to shake...

"YOU, TROLL, I ADMIRE!"

Thom opened his eyes wide in astonishment.

Wodan continued more softly.

"You showed me the respect I demand by keeping my statue safe. *AND* against all odds, you followed these men here to protect what is dear to you and your kind. You would have laid down your life for that! Your kind will be proud of you!"

The voice paused.

Wodan stood before him. The wolves lay at his feet and the ravens perched on his shoulders. He raised his spear.

"You are indeed a WARRIOR TROLL!"

Thom nearly burst with happiness.

With a crash of his spear against the rock floor of the cavern, Sleipnir, Wodan's eight-legged horse appeared, tossing its mane and stamping its hooves. Wodan mounted and, with wolves at his heels and ravens circling, Sleipnir reared upwards. The Viking god turned to Flossik and Tromsvag and cast his last words upon them:

"WODAN, ID EST FUROR!"

At last, Thom had some idea of what the words on the statue had meant. Wodan had indeed been furious.

As Sleipnir galloped away to the underworld, the two men lunged at each other and began their never-ending combat. They disappeared down the passages in the mountainside, fighting like wild beasts, and eventually their shouts and growls were lost in the distance.

Thom waited until he could hear nothing except his own breathing, coming out in short pants.

His chest swelled with pride.

He had done it!

Everything was all right! The Troll Treasure was safe! And he was still around to tell the tale!

Painfully, he got to his feet. He stopped to listen once more. The Big Men had definitely gone. And so had the drumming of Sleipnir's hooves.

But what was that faint sound?

Thom strained his ears to listen in the darkness.

A whimpering, whining came to them.

Little by little, the troll lamps re-lit and the cavern

was filled once more with a hundred colours of pastel. Then Thom saw what was making the sorrowful sound.

In a far corner, cowering and forlorn, huddled the tracker dog. His ears were flat against his head and his eyes looked over at Thom begging for kindness - something he had never experienced. He looked sad and timid. He had seen all that had happened in the cavern and it had terrified him.

It was not unusual for him to feel frightened though. Ever since he had had the misfortune to be picked as Tromsvag and Flossik's tracker dog, he had been frightened. He hoped that he would be loved if he did whatever they told him to do but it had never worked. They had still beaten him and treated him roughly. He had always been relieved to see the two men in a good mood - not that it happened often - because that meant they were not so likely to be cruel to him.

Now he lowered his head before Thom, hoping that the little troll would find it in his heart to forgive him. He was not a happy dog.

Thom did not know what to think.

Was this the same dog that had led the hated Big Men to him, chasing Grimo wildly up the path?

Was this the same dog that had bared his teeth and threatened both Thom and Hildi, preventing them from guarding their own home?

Was this the fierce tracker dog that had helped the

Big Men find the precious Troll Treasure?

Thom sighed and shook his head. For a Warrior Troll, he had a very soft heart at times. He looked over to the dog and clicked his tongue encouragingly.

The dog cocked one ear up. His eyes brightened slightly.

"Come on then..." smiled Thom, bending low and patting the ground.

The dog's tail wagged ever so slowly as if he did not dare trust Thom entirely. Thom edged forwards, keeping low so that he would not frighten the dog further, and made gentle reassuring noises. The dog shuffled forwards on his tummy, his tail now wagging pathetically and his head slightly raised.

After a few minutes of coaxing, the dog placed his head in Thom's open hands and with relief, relaxed in the knowledge that here at last was someone to care for him. Thom chuffed him under the chin and around the ears.

"Well, I'm not sure how Grimo will take it, but it looks like we've got a dog!" laughed Thom. The dog rolled over on the rocky floor so that Thom could tickle his tummy.

It was as Thom stretched out his hairy hand to do this that he noticed the statue.

It lay on its side, with Wodan's wild staring eyes looking upwards. The words were clearly visible even in the soft glow of the troll lamps.

"Wodan, id est furor."

Thom shuddered as he remembered all that he had seen and heard. That statue held great powers that he did not care to think about too much. He clicked his tongue again.

"Come on, boy, let's get out of here!" he said, picking up the statue and getting to his feet. The little troll was suddenly anxious to be in the fresh air and to feel the cold fjord water on his skin. The dog was only too pleased to do as he was told.

Together Thom and the tracker dog picked their way out of the maze of underground passages, by both memory and scent. Thom still wore his helmet. It seemed to fit his head perfectly now.

In fact, it seemed *fitting* somehow.

As Thom hurried back to the Great Cave behind the crashing waterfall, his mind raced.

He knew that he still had a matter to settle before he could return to his beloved Hildi.

Chapter 10

I t was an enormous relief to reach the Great Cave at last. The deafening crash of the ice-cold water outside was like music to Thom's ears. He and Tracker paused for a moment to catch their breath and slow their thumping hearts. They took great gulps of fresh air and stood blinking at the brightness of the sunshine that flooded the entrance to the cave. The Great Waterfall outside fell like a dazzling sheet of glass and, as they took a step nearer, Thom and Tracker could feel a fine, refreshing spray against their faces.

This felt good!

"Marvellurg!" breathed Thom to himself. It was only now that he realised that when he had set out he had not expected to see this Great Waterfall again.

His knees began to feel a little weak all of a sudden.

Tracker looked up at him, puzzled, and gave a small bark.

"Yo, yo!" replied Thom, shaking himself from his thoughts. He patted the dog on the head and the two walked to the very entrance of the Great Cave.

Peering from this high point, Thom could see the

boats on the water below. A long way down the bank, on the right, was dear Mistig Vorter. It bobbed gently in the sunshine. Thom's eyes filled with tears for a second. It was like seeing an old friend, waiting for him. It was such a temptation to run down the hill and along the bank, jump in and be off!

But just over there, on the left, was the big boat from Bergen.

This larger craft was tied with a thick rope, much closer to the Great Waterfall than his own. It had swung round to one side because of the strong current but, as Thom had suspected, was still clearly visible from the rest of the fjord. Anybody searching for the Big Men - assuming anybody cared about them - would easily find it.

This would never do.

Searching this area for Flossik and Tromsvag might lead Big People to the Troll Treasure.

Thom the Warrior Troll was not having that!

Together, Thom and Tracker made their way to the big boat. Thom still wore his helmet and he still clutched the statue tightly. It lay cold and calm in his hairy hand.

"Jump in!" Thom shouted to Tracker, as he climbed into the Bergen boat.

Tracker stayed on the bank, ears back and whined. To him, the boat stank of the cruel Big Men who used to hurt him so. He wanted nothing to do with it.

"Come on!" Thom urged, patting his knees and looking as encouraging as he could in an anxious moment. "We have to sink this boat, or else others will follow!"

On hearing these words, Tracker's ears pricked up. This sounded like a good idea! With a happy bark, he leapt aboard and stood at the stern of the boat, looking onto the fjord. His front paws were on the top rail and his back legs on the deck so that he looked brave and adventurous. The wind ruffled his fur and made his eyes water but he was proud that he had such an important job to do.

After a struggle with the thick rope's knot, Thom fell onto the deck of the boat as the current swooshed them away. It was impossible for the little troll to steer this vessel and so they had to go with the flow of the rushing water. Tracker found it exhilarating and wagged his tail furiously, but Thom, flat on his back as he was, felt slightly sick. It was a little unnerving for him to be thrown onto the deck of a boat over which he had no control.

Within a few minutes, though, the boat was floating calmly and Thom was able to get to his feet. He joined Tracker and looked back towards the Great Waterfall that had flung the boat so far into the fjord. Mistig Vorter glinted in the brilliant sunshine still tied to the bank.

"Ah, well, Tracker, nothing for it, I suppose!" smiled Thom.

Tracker looked up adoringly at Thom and thumped his tail on the deck.

Thom removed the Vendel helmet from his head and placed it carefully with the figurine of Wodan. Thom's hair was no longer spiky but flat on his head. Thom grimaced slightly as he felt it with one hairy hand - no doubt he would be teased about *this* when he got home! He took off his old, woollen jacket and green dungarees and put them down, neatly.

There he stood in all his troll-ness before Tracker.

"Tracker!" he commanded. Tracker went to him and sat at his feet. "You stay here. Sit and stay!"

And without more ado, Thom jumped overboard into the cold depths of the fjord.

Tracker's ears went down and his tail stopped wagging at this. He hoped that Thom could swim well.

Thom gasped as the icy water hit his face but he quickly started to swim, with strong troll strokes, his tail trailing in the water behind him. He was a good swimmer; he had to be, with all his fishing trips. The rowing to and from Bergen had strengthened his arms and his wide, flat troll feet were ideal to push the water with. He did not have to swim against the current of the Great Waterfall because Mistig Vorter was moored quite a way to one side of it. Thom enjoyed it.

It felt good to be fresh and cold and strong.

He soon reached the shallow water and waded to Mistig Vorter. He had never been so delighted to see his precious, loyal boat.

"Mistig! Mistig!" Thom cried as he stepped in. "Mi lovelor boot! Gooshty morgy, Mistig!"

The boat bobbed its usual greeting and the sunlight was reflected on the sides as it played on the water.

Quickly, Thom untied his boat and pushed it out into deeper water. Then, jumping in once more, he grabbed the oars and rowed out into the fjord. Ahead of him, the black shape of the Bergen boat drifted aimlessly. Tracker did not look out. He was doing just as Thom had instructed him, sitting and staying, even though the suspense was a strain for him.

Thom was greeted with great wuffs of joy as he came alongside the larger boat.

"All right, Tracker! All right!" he laughed from Mistig Vorter. "I need the moorings rope, Tracker. Do you understand? The moorings rope - go fetch!"

Tracker eagerly obeyed and appeared, front paws on the side of the boat, with the thick rope in his teeth.

"Gooshty - I mean - *good* boy!" smiled Thom. It would be a while before Tracker understood Troll-Talk. He stretched up and took hold of the rope from the dog's mouth and tied it to Mistig Vorter. The two boats were securely attached now. Then Thom carefully climbed up the rope from Mistig Vorter into the Bergen boat, where he was immediately knocked over by a madly happy dog.

"Tracker! Tracker! Calm down, boy!" Thom laughed as he shielded himself from Tracker's great welcoming licks. "We've got work to do!"

Thom began to search the large boat for a hammer or wrench or even a screwdriver - it did not matter which, really. Anything to make a big hole with.

"Go seek, Tracker!" Thom shouted and he thumped his fist on the deck of the boat to show Tracker what he wanted. "Bang! Bang!" he yelled.

Thom was getting a little anxious now. It had been quite a while since the Bergen boat had drifted into full view in the centre of the fjord. He did not want it there for long in case someone - a Big Person - saw it. He *had* to make it sink! He rummaged about, searching for a tool to help him.

Tracker barked and Thom felt a wave of relief come over him. He had found something! He went to see what it was.

A gun!

Thom hurriedly took it from the dog. "No, Tracker, not *that* sort of bang, bang!"

The dog looked disappointed and returned to where he had been searching, under some old blankets at the far end of the boat. He was not sure what to look for anymore. Thom certainly seemed frantic about something, but what? He nudged his nose against an iron bar. It fell on the wooden deck with a clang!

"GOOD BOY!" shouted Thom in delight as he saw what had made the noise. He patted Tracker on the head and rubbed his fur. "Now," Thom continued, "you go into Mistig Vorter and stay!" The dog did as he was told.

Thom cast a worried eye over the water to see if there was a sign of anyone. It bothered him to be destructive. He used to be such a gentle troll! But this he *had* to do. The Troll Treasure must never be found and neither must the evidence of this boat. After all, he thought, with a slight smile, the Big Men would not be needing their boat anymore! What was it that he had heard Wodan bellow at them?

"You shall be forever locked in deadly combat with each other! You shall NEVER escape these passages..."

Tracker barked from Mistig Vorter. Thom shook the memories away from his mind, ran down into the hold and raised the iron bar above his head.

CRACK!

The bar smacked down on the bottom of the Bergen

boat. A board began to crack.

WHACK!

The crack grew longer. A splinter of wood flew up into the air.

THWACK!

A hole had appeared in the base of the Big Men's boat.

SPLASH!

The water began to seep in. Thom thrust the iron bar into the hole he had made and rammed it backwards and forwards, making it larger. A moment later, he was hairy-ankle-deep in fjord water. He made his way up to the deck of the Big Men's boat.

One last job to do. Thom had to return Wodan to his watery grave.

Quickly, Thom picked up the figurine of Wodan and placed it, with great care and respect, inside the Vendel helmet that he had worn on his dangerous mission. He then positioned the two at the helm of the boat and took a step back.

"Thanken, thanken, Wodan! Gooshty restig, Wodan!" Thom said solemnly.

Then, with a sudden rush, the troll grabbed his sopping dungarees and jacket from the floor of the boat and jumped across to the floating safety of Mistig Vorter. He landed with a thud next to Tracker and immediately untied the rope which held the two boats together; once the big boat went down, it would drag Thom's little one with it unless he undid it fast.

Not a moment too soon!

With a wood-splintering creak and a great belching of air in water, the Bergen boat sank into the green depths of the fjord. Bubbles rose to the surface for a while, then all was still.

Wodan was at rest once more.

Back where he belonged. Not to be disturbed again.

Thom looked around him. No one was anywhere to be seen. There was only a small troll and a tracker dog in a little boat, in a great expanse of water.

The Troll Treasure was safe.

The Troll Inheritance was secure.

"Forerver Guarderig!" murmured Thom gravely, as he looked back to the Great Waterfall, both hands on the top of his head in Troll Salute.

The brilliant sunshine cheered the two travellers in Mistig Vorter. Thom's clothes, wet from the Bergen boat, soon dried. The warm breeze gently ruffled the troll's brown hair until it spiked back as it always had been. Thom strained his eyes to look into the distance, eager for the first sign of home. He could hardly believe that he had succeeded in his quest. Now, in this beautiful weather, on this beautiful water, in this beautiful boat, the horrors of the last few days seemed like a bad dream.

How was dear Hildi? Could she sense that he was safe and that all was well?

Thom was filled with a need to hold his precious troll friend to him. He wanted to feel her soft, downy hair against his cheek and to hear her gentle voice once more. He wanted to smell the herbs in their kitchen and the smoking fish over the fire.

On and on they went...

He wanted to sit in the sunshine outside his home and mend his nets, or go into the forest in search of firewood for their little stove.

On and on...

He wanted to collect his honey and paint his boat and... and...

THERE IT WAS!

There, just a short way ahead of them was Thom's landing bank. There was the little clearing in the trees where he could leave Mistig Vorter and run to Hildi!

As the boat bobbed over to the bank, Thom and Tracker leapt out and waded through the cool water, dragging on Mistig Vorter's moorings rope. Then, with fast steps, the two of them raced up the woodland path, home.

The door was wide open, letting the warm sun in. The red and white checked curtains blew' gently in the slight breeze and there was a smell of freshly baked rye bread floating on the air.

Thom slowed his pace as he came to the door. He could hear the clattering of pots in the kitchen and the familiar squeaks of the mice. He stood still outside, not wanting to burst in and shock Hildi.

"Hildi?" he called gently.

It all went quiet in the kitchen.

"Hildi? Im homerig! Es Thom!" Thom called.

There was a sudden SMASH as the pots fell from Hildi's hand. Then a shout of joy and Hildi rushed out of the door, straight into Thom's outstretched arms. They hugged and hugged each other, not wanting to let go.

"Mi Thom!" Hildi gasped at last. "Mi lovelor Thom! Kissig, kissig!" And the trolls embraced once more.

"For goodness' sake! Get a grip on yourselves, will you?" came a disgusted squeak from the doorstep. Tailo was delighted to see Thom safely home, but all this open expression of love embarrassed him beyond measure.

"Now you leave them alone!" squawked Scratchen, scampering up to the other mouse to see what was happening. "They've got a lot of kissing to catch up on!"

Hildi and Thom turned, laughing, to look at the mice.

"Gooshty morgy, morsies!" Thom greeted them.

Tailo tutted and turned indoors. Scratchen followed. It was good that Thom was home - now things could get back to normal. Even Tailo being unpleasant would be good; he had been far too nice recently; he was getting boring to live with.

Tracker, who had been sitting a little way down the path, whined quietly. He wanted to join in with the excitement but knew not to move until Thom told him to do so.

Now, Thom beckoned him, telling Hildi that here was a true and loyal friend. Tracker wagged his tail madly as he was accepted gently into the trolls' home.

Grimo arrived later. After a quick swipe of a well-aimed paw, the pecking order was soon established. THAT DOG was not *too* bad as long as he knew his place - and stuck to it.

And so, that evening, as the sun set, dipping its orange fingers into the dark waters of the fjord, the trolls sat in their little kitchen once more. The cuckoo clock, tick - tick - ticked quietly and the animals snoozed in the warmth of the fire.

Once more, Hildi and Thom were peaceful. They turned to smile at each other. They were filled with smoked fish, bilberries and nettle tea.

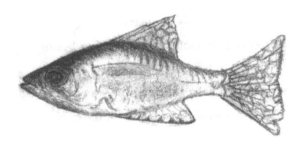

And with happiness.
And with love.
Just like it had always been.